OPERATION GREEN CARD

WITHDRAWN

G.B. GORDON

RIPTIDE
PUBLISHING

Riptide Publishing
PO Box 1537
Burnsville, NC 28714
www.riptidepublishing.com

Operation Green Card

Cover art: L.C. Chase, lcchase.com/design.htm
Editors: Sarah Lyons, Carole-ann Galloway
Layout: L.C. Chase, lcchase.com/design.htm

ISBN: 978-1-62649-676-7

First edition
December, 2017

Also available in ebook:
ISBN: 978-1-62649-675-0

OPERATION GREEN CARD

G.B. GORDON

RIPTIDE
PUBLISHING

Because love is love.

TABLE OF CONTENTS

"**C**'mon, I tried," Jason said to the *It's-so-fluffy* unicorn belted in on the passenger seat beside him.

The unicorn was clearly not impressed. Jason didn't blame it. He'd tried to leave work early, but he wasn't sure if that stuff just never worked out as planned or if his subconscious was always planning against him. On the plus side, it had made the drive from Bluewater Bay to Seattle a breeze, because he was hours behind the rush-hour traffic. But it also meant it was past ten by the time he reached Highland Park, and when he pulled up to the curb, the little rental under the big trees was predictably dark.

He turned to the unicorn. "Looks like you'll be spending the night on the porch, buddy."

The unicorn was glaring at him and sticking its tongue out.

Jason sighed and looked back toward the house. He'd known Lily would be in bed before he made it. Of course he had. But he'd hoped he'd at least be able to have a peek at her as she slept.

With a sigh, he unbuckled his belt and the unicorn's, then awkwardly climbed out of the car, dragging the big plushy and getting his dummy foot stuck inside the doorframe.

"Jason?"

He turned and almost fell flat on his face, but caught one hand on the frame at the last second.

Kendra stood in the half-open front door, outlined against the hall light, a trash bag dangling against her leg.

Jason hooked one hand behind his knee and pulled the trapped foot free.

"Sorry it got so late. I wasn't going to ring the bell, I swear." He held out the unicorn. "I was just going to leave him on the porch."

She didn't look a day older than she had that fateful night six years ago, the week before he'd gotten himself deployed. Tall and athletic, though the weak light made her edges softer. She brushed a strand of hair behind her ear. "Do you want to come in? Let me just get rid of this."

He waited until she'd crammed the bag into the trash can by the side of the house, then followed her inside. "Dan not home?'

"He's on night shift this week. He left about an hour ago." She led him into the kitchen, where he plopped the unicorn into a chair.

"Cute," she said. "Did you see the movie?"

"Just clips, but the little girl reminded me of Lily. I thought she might enjoy it."

"She'll love it. She asks about you. Wants to know what your favorite ice cream is. Stuff like that. C'mon, Jay, just take her out for ice cream one of these days. At least come over when she's awake. Too often, you come when she's already in bed."

He tried not to pull his head between his shoulders. Guilty as charged. But he wasn't good for Lily. Better to leave things as they were. "I don't want to confuse her."

"Bull," Kendra said without heat. "She understands very well Dan adopted her, and who you are. You know that." She stuck her tongue out at him. "I showed her your yearbook picture." Then she got serious again. "Kids aren't that easily confused. And Lily's smarter than most." There was pride in her face when she smiled. "She had to have a pre-admission screening for kindergarten because her birthday was after the cut-off date, and they told us she's gifted."

"Wow." On the surface, it was what every parent wanted to hear, but it also made him wary. It meant his little girl was different. And different meant difficult. It always did. "Does that mean a special school for her?"

Kendra shrugged. "They mentioned that as a possibility, but a grand a month? Who can afford that, right? But there are programs at school, and she might skip a grade later on." She cocked her head at him. Reading some of his doubts in his face, maybe? "She'll be fine, Jay. She's an absolute joy. You really need to visit during the day."

Too close. He was only good for people at a distance. He'd have no idea what to say to her, what to do, how to keep her happy. The only way he knew how to do that was by helping Kendra and Dan with whatever money he could spare. Kendra had balked at it at first. They didn't need it, Dan had a good job, she'd said. But Jason had a pretty good idea what Dan earned at the steel mill. It might be a steady income, but it sure as hell wouldn't be stellar. And he himself didn't need much. Kendra had only relented when he'd suggested investing the money in a GET program for Lily's college.

"Do you want to see her?" Kendra asked.

It would cost him, but he did. So much. "Yeah, I . . . If you think . . ."

"Come on upstairs."

At the top of the stairs she put a finger to her lips, then eased open the door to Lily's room and waved him in.

Lily lay sprawled sideways on her mattress, one fist tangled up in the cloud of dark curls spilling across the sheets, the other wrapped around a small and decidedly limp bunny, the blankets in a puddle on the floor. She had grown since he'd last seen her, her limbs longer now, less babyish. But she was still so tiny.

She made his throat tight and set off all kinds of weird shit in his chest. He'd known this would happen. She did that to him every damned time. He wasn't sure why he did that to himself, why he kept coming back here. Except that he needed to. She tethered him. Even though he didn't belong here, he belonged to her in a way. Without her, he'd be completely adrift.

He didn't know how long he stood, just looking at his sleeping daughter, but when he turned back toward the door, Kendra had left.

He found her downstairs in the kitchen, where she'd poured herself some milk.

"Can I get you anything?" She pointed at the fridge. "Do you want a beer?"

Jason shook his head. "Driving. I should get home too. Early day tomorrow." He paused, not sure how to get out what was sticking in his brain about the school she'd mentioned and how much it cost. It wasn't his call. And he didn't have the money either. He'd try to get it, of course, but better not talk about that unless he actually had something to talk about.

"Drive safe."

"Always."

"Jay?"

He was already in the hallway and looked back over his shoulder.

"Think about coming by when she's up. You know you're always welcome."

"Yeah. Thanks. I will." *Think about it.*

He threw a last glance at the unicorn, then left. It was a long drive back to Bluewater Bay.

It was just that bit harder to get up before dawn the next day, and Jason was grateful that Mark, his ride-share and *Wolf's Landing's* head of costumes, wasn't a talker. Traffic was light this early, but Jason's tired brain was stuck in a loop of *She's gifted. She needs a special school. I can't afford it. But, she's gifted.* He didn't have room in there for chitchat.

Jason threw a glance to his right. They weren't friends. Close to; Mark might be the closest thing to a friend he had, but it was easier this way. Friendship always seemed to require talking about oneself, which he wasn't good at. And eventually people left, which was harder. So yeah, this was fine.

At the *Wolf's Landing* studios, the gate opened when they arrived. Turner, who was on duty this morning, peered inside the car and waved when they went past the brightly lit gate house, but he'd already opened the gate on their approach, when he could only have recognized the car. Convenient, but not safe. Jason filed it away to bring up as a general point at the next weekly meeting. It wasn't his place to discipline anyone.

He automatically scanned the parking lot when he got out. One of the cameras seemed a little out of alignment. He'd better check that on the monitor.

Mark had already wandered off, so Jason locked the car and made his way over to the tower, which was what the guys had dubbed the surveillance center. It wasn't an elevated structure at all, merely a room filled with monitors and communication equipment on the second floor of the administration building. Jason assumed the semicircular arrangement of the larger monitors had reminded someone of an airport traffic control tower. He had no idea where the name would otherwise have come from.

He went through the routine of shift change, glanced through the log, then poured himself a coffee from his thermos and settled in. The studio never really slept, but it did quiet down over night. Now the early birds trickled in.

He watched one of the producers, Anna Maxwell, drive in, always among the first to arrive and one of the last to leave, Jeremy like a magnet on her tail. Now there was a detail that would pay him more money than babysitting the fucking monitors did, but they'd never let him work as a bodyguard. Would they? He could at least ask; worst that could happen was a no. He knew he'd be good at it. *Don't get your hopes up, Cooley.*

The camera of Parking Three was indeed a bit off. He was missing a corner of the lot on his screen. It didn't happen often, but occasionally a large bird of prey or an adventurous raccoon could move a camera, if it wasn't fastened tight. He'd see if he could catch Krueger in his office after lunch and let him know. Jason could just write it into the shift log, but he wanted to talk to Krueger anyway. He hated asking for anything, but he really needed to make more money. *She's gifted. She needs a special school.*

He sighed and unpacked a sandwich. Another boring day, courtesy of a missing limb that disqualified him from what he wanted or was good at. He stared at his left shoe: not even anything in there he could hate. He didn't hate the prosthesis; he'd be worse off without it. And one couldn't hate air.

Damn, wasn't it lunchtime yet?

Jason knocked on the frame of the open door and stepped into his boss's office. He waited until Krueger had finished his phone call, then said, "One of the cameras in parking lot three is off-kilter. Might want to send someone out with a ladder."

Krueger nodded. "Thanks. And you're really here, because . . ."

Damn, the bastard didn't miss a thing. Ever. Jason took a deep breath. "I need another shift."

Krueger blinked. "You're kidding, right?"

"Nope."

"Is there something going on I should know about? Anything I can help with? You're not in any trouble, are you? What in the world do you need all that money for?"

All that money. When they were paying him a dollar above minimum wage.

"Price of bread is rising again," Jason deadpanned to stop the questions.

"Yeah, fuck you too."

Shit. He hated standing here, begging for work. But he couldn't afford to antagonize the guy, who'd been trying to be nice.

"My daughter's tuition just went up."

Immediately Krueger relented. "That sucks, man. I have two. Twelve and fourteen. I hear ya. But honestly, Cooley, I don't know what you expect me to do. You're already working two shifts and the day only has three. Are you sleeping on weekends only, or what?"

Jason chewed on his cheek. "I could work weekends. Or at least let me switch one shift for night." Night shift paid a buck more per hour.

"I don't have any openings. Best I can do is let you have first dibs when someone's sick."

Jason nodded. "Appreciate it." He turned to leave, then stopped. "Unless you want to put me on a close-protection detail."

Krueger groaned. "Cooley, you're killing me, you know that? You want to work as a bodyguard? With your medical?"

The anger flared up like a match struck in his gut. "Fuck the medical. I pass the fitness test every year. And you know as well as I do that I could run circles around at least two of the guys out there. Not because I run faster, but because I'd be moving before it even registered on their two brain cells that something was happening."

"I know, I know. Unfortunately that's not the point. Point is, regs. If I signed off on the guy with one leg doing anything except sitting in a chair monitoring the surveillance equipment, we'd both be out of a job."

Jason pressed both fists against his thighs in an effort to rein in his temper, and Krueger sighed.

"I don't know what to tell you, Cooley. Buy a lottery ticket, marry rich, or, seriously, go back to school for higher paying work; you're a smart guy. I'd hate to lose you, but I can give you some contacts if you want to go that way."

"Thanks," Jason got out. "I'll think about it."

It wasn't Krueger's fault. The guy was trying his best. But that still left Jason empty-handed. And seething. Easy for the shrinks at the hospital to tell him that losing his leg didn't define who he was. Tell that to everyone else. Because it sure as hell defined who he *wasn't* anymore.

He did a sharp about turn and left the office, almost colliding with Natalya, the stunt coordinator, in the hallway. He'd seen her around a few times, but they hadn't really talked much. And, of course, the whole studio knew about her relationship with Anna Maxwell, the producer. It had been impossible to miss at the time; the gossip machine had made sure of that, though things had quietened down. With a mumbled apology he brushed past her, surprised when she fell into step beside him, or tried to.

She only reached to about his chest and had to run to keep up with his stride. "Damn it, slow down a minute, would you?"

"Why?" He was still pissed, but not at her, of course, and curiosity was starting to gain the upper hand, so he relented and shortened his step. Less of an effort, anyway, but the whole thing had been satisfying for about five seconds.

"I couldn't help overhearing the tail end of your conversation when I passed. I might have an idea for you."

"That was private," he growled.

"Sorry. You were loud. You want to hear it or not?" She spoke with a hard Russian accent, and her eyes dared him to mess with her, even though she had to look up quite a ways.

He hadn't calmed down enough to find the humor in that, but she had his attention. "Fine. Shoot."

"Not here. The Gull. Tonight. You know it? Does 8 p.m. work for you?"

The Gull? Really? She was avoiding his eyes, which made this whole thing sound even more suspicious. "If it involves drugs, I'm not interested."

"What? No!"

"Is it legal?"

Again her eyes slid to the side, then she threw him a mischievous grin. "Maybe not exactly, but something like moonlighting doesn't sound so bad, does it?"

He clicked his tongue, thinking. Maybe she did have something for him. He could still walk away if he didn't like it. "Make it nine, and I'll be there."

He got a brief nod in response, then she turned and disappeared down the hallway to his left. He stared after her for a few seconds, then made his way toward the stairs. Elevators were for pussies. And fuck his old drill sergeant for making him hear that in his voice.

Jason had quickly dropped off Mark and taken ten to shower and change out of his uniform.

He went to the Gull for a pint or a few now and then. It was a somewhat dingy little relic of Bluewater Bay's pre-TV days. One beer on tap, one bottled import brand. The menu consisted of a large jar of pickled eggs and a bowl of peanuts on the bar. It was a good place if one wanted to get quietly shit-faced in a corner. And an excellent choice if Natalya didn't want anyone to know about their meeting. Jason had never seen any of the Hollywood crew here, and he didn't know any of the locals. He was surprised Natalya had even heard of the place. She didn't strike him as the type who got quietly shit-faced all by her lonely self.

Right now she was waiting for him at a small table in the corner by the door, tapping her foot and drumming her fingers.

When she saw him, she slapped her hand on the table in what looked very much like triumph. It didn't help Jason's feeling that he might be getting himself in over his head. He grabbed a pint at the bar, then joined her, watching all the little tell-tale signs of her nervousness—the tapping, lip biting, roaming eyes. Well, keeping her off-kilter until he knew what she wanted worked in his favor, so he didn't say anything, merely kept observing. She was cute, and nicely muscled, but he preferred his women tall and dark-haired. Cute wasn't going to get her a break.

She took a sip of beer, then set the glass back down. "So, you came."

He had, but not to make small talk. The sooner he knew what the hell she wanted, the better. "You have something to say, say it."

"You need money," she shot at him, niceties definitely over. "Why?"

"None of your business."

She leaned back and fiddled with a beer mat until it snapped in half between her fingers. "What I have in mind involves someone else," she said. "But before I bring him in on this, I need to know that you're not in trouble with the law."

He laughed. "Really? *You* need to know that *I'm* not in trouble? After going through all this shady stuff?" He waved around at the cigarette-yellow walls and ceiling.

There was that saucy grin again. He was getting an idea of what Anna saw in her. It was conspiratorial and engaging, a daredevil grin.

"Humor me."

"I'm not in trouble."

She seemed to weigh that for a moment, then dug for her wallet and pulled out a faded and dog-eared picture. For a few seconds she stared at it without a word, then handed it to him.

It showed two young men, one blond, one dark-haired, both lanky, almost skinny, arms around each other's shoulders, smiling and waving into the camera.

Jason put the picture faceup on the table and watched her, waiting for an explanation.

"That," her finger tapped the blond one, "is my brother Arkady. That," tap, tap on the other man, "was his best friend, Dimitri. They weren't a couple, though they're both gay. Dimitri died while they were in the army under mysterious circumstances about a year after this picture was taken. Because that's what happens to gay men in

Russia." She threw him a challenging glance. "He was nineteen. That was ten years ago. The situation is worse today."

There wasn't really anything to say beyond the obvious outrage, so he didn't.

After a while she went on, "I've been trying to get Arkady out of Russia since I came here, but it's never been more pressing than in the past few years. Ever since Putin's Propaganda Laws—" She choked on whatever she was going to say, and took a hasty gulp from her glass. "He was supposed to get hired by security on the set last winter, but it fell through. He needs a green card yesterday."

Again she paused, but Jason was still mystified. She'd overheard him asking for more work. Why would she think he could help with a job for her brother?

"Something Ben Krueger said when you left his office . . ." Her hand closed into a fist on the table, opened and closed, opened and closed. "I've tried everything else." It was a whisper, as if she was trying to convince herself this was a good idea.

The good idea for *him* might be to get up and walk away now.

"When Krueger joked about you needing to marry rich, I had this thought."

What?

"I know people are marrying for green cards, so it must work."

"Come again?"

"You need money. I know Arkady has some savings I'm sure he'd be willing to invest in getting out of Russia. I'll have to talk to him, but he could also share whatever he earns with you as soon as he finds work."

"Whoa. Hold it. Are you asking me to marry your brother?"

"It's legal now."

"That's the most . . . I'm not even gay."

At that she barked a bitter laugh. "Really? That's your objection to a fake marriage? That you're not gay?"

The shame washed over him like acid. It wasn't even like he thought that would be particularly terrible. Hell, he very much doubted there was a soldier out there with long-term deployment under his belt who'd had zero contact with another man's dick. In any case, it had been a stupid thing to say. "Sorry."

She got up. "You know what? Forget it. You're not the kind of guy I should have as—"

"Every other objection was obvious, so why would I mention them?"

"What?"

"That it's illegal? That it can fail at about fifty different stages? That he might not even want to take the chance? You know all that."

She paused, half-standing, both hands on the table.

And against all reason, it suddenly became most important to convince her that she was wrong about him. "I don't give a shit about anyone being gay or not. It just seemed like a thing one would want to know in a situation like this."

It wasn't a lie, though it sounded more thought-out than it had been; he hadn't quite gotten to the bottom of where he stood on that line. This whole proposition had come way too far out of left field.

Natalya sat back down, but she didn't stop frowning at him.

He picked the picture up again and stared at the blond guy, a boy, really. Okay, ten years ago, so he was a man now. Still. He didn't deserve to be harassed or hurt or, worse, killed for who he loved or fucked. Nobody did.

"Does that mean you'll do it?" Natalya asked.

"I don't know. It's not the kind of decision I want to make over a beer. I don't have the foggiest idea how this would work and what it would entail. Why don't you ask your brother if he'd even consider it?" After all, it might be a decision he wouldn't have to make. It was such a desperately ludicrous thing to do. The more he thought about it, the more he was sure this Arkady would give his sister a piece of his mind about what she said to random strangers.

"Okay. Yeah, I'll talk to him." She sounded deflated now, robbed of momentum, and he took the opportunity to drain his glass.

"I guess I'll see you around, then."

She nodded without words, eyes fixed on the photograph on the table. So he left, pulled his collar up against the April wind, and walked back to the house by the beach that had been his grandmother's. Snippets of their discussion ricocheted around in his skull. The boy who'd been killed. The other one who was in danger. Neither one of them was any of his business, really. He was under no obligation to save anyone. He didn't know the guy. Hell, he barely knew Natalya.

He knew himself, though. And walking away just wasn't in his DNA. Getting people out of danger zones was what he did. What he'd been trained for, anyway, though these days his job was more about preventing visitors from "getting lost" on set. Was this the universe throwing him a bone? A chance to do something that would actually make a difference to someone? He took a deep breath and let it out slowly.

Then there was the money. However much *some savings* was. He could definitely use money, but robbing a man of his life savings wasn't his thing. And a second income only sounded tempting if it wasn't hypothetical. Would the guy be allowed to work in the first place?

Ah, fuck, it was bullshit even to think about the whole plan, because Natalya's brother would want to know what she was smoking. There was no way anyone would agree to this. He should put it out of his mind and figure out how he could come up with a better paying shift.

With that resolution firmly in place, he fired up his computer as soon as he got home to google *green card marriage*.

CHAPTER TWO

The rock came out of nowhere and hit Arkady just under his cheekbone with enough force to whip his head around. He instinctively ducked down on one knee, but was too startled to form coherent thought. The street seemed completely empty in the semidarkness of false dawn. He was in the wrong part of town for a mugging, hadn't even crossed the river yet. Kids, then? Leftover partiers out for a drunken lark?

"*Pidar.*" The hiss came from the left. Though all Arkady saw was a low stone wall, the homophobic slur sent his heartbeat up into his throat. *Fuck!* It meant the attack hadn't been random. But how so? Who? He'd been afraid of something like this ever since the university had fired him, but this was a terrifying first. Was this a student? An ex-colleague? Or had the rumors that he was gay spread beyond the university by now?

As he slowly approached the wall, he heard cursing and twigs snapping. He should probably run, but he couldn't help himself. The need to see the face behind the hatred and the rock pushed him forward. He kept his forearm up, expecting another rock, but nothing happened, and when he rounded the corner where the wall met a low fence, all he found was some crushed grass and an empty bottle.

He went back to where he'd dropped his tool bag on the sidewalk, dug his cigarettes out of the side pocket, and lit one with shaking fingers. The whole left side of his face throbbed with every beat of his heart, but careful probing with his tongue revealed no broken teeth. The metallic taste of blood told him he'd cut his cheek on his own teeth, though.

That had been too close. Much too close to home. Too close in every respect. Whoever had been behind that wall had been waiting there, had known Arkady would pass here on his way to work, had known who he was.

It took a second cigarette before he calmed down enough to get going again, to the small electric company that was work these days, and to face cousin Misha—who was also his boss—and his concerned scrutiny.

"You're late, Sparky."

Arkady turned barely enough to give his cousin the finger, before dropping his tool bag on the shop floor and stretching his shoulders. Normally he shrugged the hated nickname off, but this morning he was already done.

"*Pizdets*! What the fuck happened to your face?" Misha came over and gently hooked his finger under Arkady's chin, turning his left cheek into the light.

"Probably looks worse than it is."

"Your fucking cheek's cut open, man."

Arkady winced and jerked his head back. "I'd better get cleaned up, then." He should reassure Misha, make light of the truth, or invent a kind lie, but he didn't have the energy or the head space. He ducked into the tiny washroom and inspected his face in the mirror. Yeah, it wasn't pretty, but the cut wasn't deep and had stopped bleeding. An open cut might even save him from developing the grandmother of all bruises. He slid the first aid kit off the shelf by the door and braced himself for the disinfectant. *Blyat*, that crap stung. The sticking plasters in the kit were all too short to cover the cut, so he left it. He was scheduled to work on a building site today, and he didn't need the shit he'd get from construction workers for putting an actual bandage on a shallow cut. A quip about women with long nails would have to do to head off any questions.

He volunteered for grunt duty, laying cables, just to be able to work alone that day, but it was a double-edged sword, because it gave him ample time to think. About really having to leave now, like Tasha'd been telling him all along. Leave Petersburg, the city he loved; leave everything behind. And not "eventually," as he'd anticipated a year ago, when he'd lost his job and lost every chance at making full professor. But the worst, leave his family: Misha and Katya and the girls, his parents, his aunt and uncle . . . Merely thinking about it felt like a fist around his heart. A very different pain from a little cut on his cheek.

His stomach was rumbling when he finished up and stepped out for a smoke on the concrete platform that was going to be the fifth floor of the building. Checking his watch told him he'd not only missed lunch, but was working overtime. He needed a shower and something to eat.

When he returned to the shop and hung the keys for the truck up on the board, Misha came over and wrapped an arm around his shoulders. "You okay, Sparky?"

"Yeah, yeah. Just beat. Crawling around in hip-high spaces dragging a cable drum all day will do that to you." *Plus, I'm not a fucking electrician, I'm a literature docent, and I'd much rather teach Chekhov and Shakespeare.* But that last part, he didn't say, because he owed Misha. For giving him a job, for supporting Arkady in every way. Hell, working here had put him through university in the first place.

"I guess you don't want to hear about Pavel's freezer crapping out again, then?"

"Fuuuck. When's he going to replace that piece of shit?" Arkady picked his tool bag up again, but Misha took it from him.

"I've got this. Go home, Kashka. Sleep. You've been on for ten hours straight now, and knowing you, you didn't eat."

"Guilty."

"See you tomorrow. Or better, have dinner with us."

Normally he'd jump at the idea: great food, playing with the girls . . . But tonight it would just remind him of all the things he couldn't have. All happy families were indeed alike. He hadn't asked to be different. Alike would have worked fine for him, thankyouverymuch.

"Not tonight. Rain check?"

Misha gave him a long, hard stare, but then dropped it with a shrug. "Okay, see you tomorrow, then."

"Thanks, Misha. I appreciate it. All of it."

"Get out of here, Sparky."

This time Arkady managed a grin. It pulled on the cut. "Asshole."

Misha's laughter followed him out the door.

April was preparing for May with a real effort at spring, and for a few minutes, Arkady stopped on the bridge across the Nevka to admire the shades-of-apricot beauty reflected on the water and let the evening sunshine drive the dark clouds out of his head. It had been a long day, was all. He was alive, he had a job, and when he got home, there would be mail from America waiting for him, asking him to pack his bags.

Which was what he'd been half-dreading, half-hoping every day for over a year now, ever since Tasha had told him the film people had promised a job and papers. It would happen. Eventually. When the sun was shining on him and glinting off the water like this, he could almost see a day when he wouldn't have to live a lie anymore; when he'd be able to have a family of his own.

He spit into the river below, because when you were leaning over the banister of a bridge and didn't feel the urge to spit into the water, you were practically dead and calcified already. Then he pushed himself off the banister and squinted into the low evening sun. Despite the late hour it was still too bright to make out the silhouette of the fortress on the other side. A promise of the white nights to come.

Turning away from the Petrogradskaya embankment, he did a quick shoulder check and immediately hated himself for it. The rock at dawn had shaken him worse than he cared to admit, but deep down he'd felt on thin ice since the university had fired him. They hadn't actually accused him of being gay, of course—not to his face. They didn't have anything concrete. He'd been extremely careful, had avoided the muscled and ultra-male tough guys he had such a weak spot for, and this past year, he'd avoided any sort of relationship at all.

But the university hadn't been able to give him a solid reason for firing him either. He knew the budget cuts line had been a lie. And he knew the looks and the whispers and the occasional verbal challenge. Rumors had followed him like shadows for years. A decade, even. Had followed him since Mitja's death. It had only been a question of time until they caught up with him.

And if he wasn't allowed to work with university students in Petersburg, the most liberal of Russian cities, he'd never work in a university again. Not in Russia. Not unless they needed an electrician.

But that was no reason to live like a mouse. He wasn't important enough for anyone to care about who and what he was as long as he lay low, which meant he didn't need to check over his shoulder. Or so he'd thought until this morning.

Maybe he was already listed and being watched, and had been since his time in the army. But then nothing he did now, short of giving them an obvious excuse, would make a difference anyway.

When he unlocked the battered door to his building, it took an effort not to look over his shoulder again. Too many rumors, a rock too close to home, and Mitja.

He checked for mail with his usual vow to give up smoking and cut down on his drinking for the right letter, bracing himself for the disappointment, but it still hit him low and hard, every day. No envelope with Latin letters in the bunch.

He dragged himself up the stairs and into the tiny bedsit he'd been living in since his graduate days. At least he still had that. At least, with the job Misha gave him, he could still live close to the university, in the midst of clubs and cafés, art and books.

He showered and checked his email, frowning at a message from Tasha to *Call me. Anytime.*

It was just after five now, so early in the morning for her. Normally he would wait a bit to give her a chance to coffee up, but the *anytime* gave him the fidgets. He logged in to Skype and watched the call go unanswered, lit a cigarette, then tried again. Now she answered, bleary-eyed, definitely pre-coffee. She put a finger to her lips, and the blur behind her told him she was walking with her phone. Probably trying not to wake Anna.

"Hey," she said, when the kitchen cabinets appeared behind her. "Did you just get home?"

"About half an hour ago, but I just saw your email." His stomach was coiled in a complicated knot of hope and trepidation. "Any news?"

"Maybe. I don't know. I had this idea. But it might be a little too wild, even for us." She grinned, and the coil slid firmly toward hope.

"I'm listening."

She tugged at her hair for a moment, then said in a rush, "There's a guy at work who may be willing to marry you for a green card in exchange for money." She took a deep breath.

Arkady blinked. "What?"

"Think about it, Kashka. It's legal here, now. It would be the perfect solution. You can come for a vacation, meet the guy; if he rubs you the wrong way, you fly back, nothing lost."

He took a breath to reply, but she cut in.

"I'll pay for the ticket. If you decide to stay, you can get married, file your papers, and have all the time in the world to find a job. It'll be so much easier than trying to find one long-distance."

This time she paused, clearly waiting for an answer. He didn't have one. The green card marriage was hardly a new idea, of course. For a woman. He tried to push through the tangle of preconceptions in his head. Regardless of gender, it had always struck him as a desperate solution. So many unknowns of helplessness and dependencies. Was he that desperate? Today? Maybe.

"What's he like, this guy at work?"

Tasha let out a long breath. "He seems like a decent guy. Ex-soldier, works security on set. He lost a leg in . . ." She frowned. "I don't actually know where, and I probably should have asked. Anyway, a veteran. He's been hustling for more work, and not getting any, so he needs money."

Suspicion was like a shark fin slicing through the waters of his musings. "What for?"

Again the frown. "Nothing illegal."

"You don't know."

"No, I don't. But I believe him. Look, I don't know the guy all that well, but my gut says to trust him. And my gut isn't all that generous that way."

He huffed a laugh. That was an understatement if he'd ever heard one. Where Natalya Nikolayevna trusted, he was inclined to follow. Still . . .

"What the hell did you do to your face?"

He'd been sitting with his left side away from the light, but must have shifted. *Shit.* "Nothing. Don't worry about it."

"Nothing? You look like you got into a fight. Did you?"

"No, nothing that dramatic. I ran into a rock, but it was a craven, half-assed thing, and it's over now. There's nothing you can do, so stop worrying, okay?"

"*Khuinya*. I know there's a big part of you that doesn't want to leave. And I know it's a weird thing to suggest—"

"I mean, what sort of a man marries for money?"

"Think about it at least? I have to wait to hear back from him anyway. He hasn't said yes yet. But he hasn't said no either." She stared past her phone screen for a second, then looked back at him. "I prefer that to someone jumping at the chance."

He blew a smoke ring. "I guess."

"I'm not asking you to sign any vows right now, Arkady. Just come and meet the guy. Then make up your mind. Besides, I wouldn't mind seeing you." Her voice had grown soft on the last words, making his throat tight.

"I miss you too. How are things with you and Anna?"

"Good. Really good." Her wide, happy smile was easily the best thing he'd seen all day. They chatted for a few minutes longer, then logged off. Arkady sat staring at her name on the screen until his stomach growled and the cigarette burned his fingers.

He stubbed it out, put the kettle on, and threw a pack of Rollton noodles into a bowl with soy sauce and hot sauce.

Marry a stranger for a green card? He wasn't seriously thinking about that, was he? And an ex-soldier? He shook his head to silence Mitja's voice warning him off. He'd never be rid of that voice. They'd gone to school together, and discovering they were both gay had thrown them together, despite their differences. They'd learned together, haunted the cafés and later bars together. They'd shared pretty much everything except a bed. It hadn't been that kind of a relationship. They'd been too different. Mitja had been loud and proud, where Arkady was contemplative and careful.

They'd been so stupid when they were drafted. They believed in a modern Russia, a changing Russia, and they were eighteen and invulnerable. He could still hear Mitja's enthusiastic remarks about *this guy's ass* and how the lieutenant *would look better out of uniform*.

They'd come for Mitja on a snowy Monday morning about 4 a.m., the day before Arkady's nineteenth birthday, and had dragged him out of his bunk. Arkady would have gone after them, except for Pasha holding him in a bear hug that had broken two of his ribs because he'd struggled against it until he couldn't breathe anymore.

The kettle whistled, making him jump and bang his knuckles against the counter. He sucked on his fist while pouring the hot water over the noodles. A can of sliced mushrooms and a generous dollop of sour cream completed his dinner. He took the bowl over to the couch and opened his tattered and heavily annotated copy of *Catch-22*, but put it down again when he caught himself staring into space after only five lines. Not the right book to take his mind off Mitja.

When Pasha had finally let him go, Arkady had found that he'd broken the big guy's nose with the back of his head. It had taken him years to acknowledge that there was nothing he could have done. Pasha had probably saved his life. At the point he'd admitted that to himself, he'd been unable to track the man down to apologize.

His stomach roiled at the flood of memories, and he set his noodles back on the table, only half-eaten. Instead, he opened the new bottle of vodka he'd saved for an emergency and proceeded to quietly and determinedly get drunk. So drunk, he could stop thinking about the mess his life was, in a country where he'd never have a family and kids. Even if by some miracle he found a tough guy who did turn out to be the family type. So drunk, he could stop thinking about leaving his home and his family, and whether he wanted to marry a stranger to do it.

He was still banging his brain against that question through his hangover the next morning, and through the rest of the week until Tasha called him back on Saturday.

"He said yes," she announced without preamble.

"What?" Arkady knew what she meant, of course, but his mind felt stupid and sluggish and raw. He was no closer to a decision than he'd been three days ago.

"Jason. The guy at work. He agreed to meet you." She paused.

"He did?" Arkady asked, just to fill the silence.

"He did. And the money isn't for anything illegal."

"He says?"

"Yeah, well. Like I said, check him out, make up your own mind."

"Is he gay?"

"Jesus Christ. Men. What the hell does that have to do with it? Do you want to fuck the guy or get your papers?"

"No. Yeah. You're right. Perfectly."

"Arkady?"

He squeezed his eyes shut. Wanted to tell her, *Never mind.* Or change the topic. Talk of something else.

"Where's your sense of adventure, Kashka?"

Died in an army barracks ten years ago. But he didn't say that. Mainly because as he opened his mouth, he knew with sudden, blinding clarity that if he said no now, he would beat himself up over his cowardice for the rest of his life.

"Plotting exit strategies," he said instead.

Her voice turned instantly jubilant. "You'll come? When?"

He mentally reviewed how long it would take him to wrap up his life. "How about summer? There are things I have to take care of."

"Okay." Her impatience cut the word short. "Keep me posted?"

"Always. I'll probably send you some of my stuff. That okay?"

"Stupid question. Sure it is. Anytime. You know that."

He wanted to hug her, but he also wanted to log off and get started. Having made the decision flooded him with unexpected energy that had nowhere to go.

"I do. Gotta run. Talk to you soon."

Misha took one look at him when he showed up at work on Monday, and raised both eyebrows in an unspoken query.

Arkady ignored it. If anyone asked questions or interrogated his friends and family when he was gone, he didn't want Misha to have to lie. On the other hand, he couldn't just disappear and leave Misha in the lurch. A compromise, then.

"Tasha sends her love," he said, while dealing with his paperwork from Friday.

"How is she?"

"Pretty happy. But she says she misses me. I might visit her for a couple of weeks this summer."

He didn't turn to look at his cousin, but the silence behind him spoke eloquently of Misha's putting two and two together.

"A couple of weeks, huh?"

"Yeah." Arkady kept his voice level. "Think you can spare me for maybe two or three weeks?"

"Sure." There was a brief pause, then Misha said, "Might have to hire someone."

He'd apparently come up with four. His cousin had always been good at math.

"Might have to."

That was all they said about it. All they needed to say.

Arkady packed up his best-loved books and some personal items and sent his sister a handful of packages, judiciously spaced out over the next few weeks.

He'd sent her his savings for safekeeping when the university fired him, and been sending whatever money he didn't need for rent or food ever since, even though the security job hadn't panned out. Because he'd known for a long time that he needed to leave. Didn't mean he had to like it.

At the end of May, he went to visit his parents and tell them of his upcoming vacation. They seemed happy for him and gave him messages of love for Natalya, but when he left, his father hugged him goodbye hard, and his mother laid her hand on his head like a blessing. They knew.

Tasha booked him on a Lufthansa flight via Frankfurt to Seattle for the end of June, and sent him his return-ticket confirmation and a written invitation for his visa application. Misha wrote him a letter of employment.

Arkady didn't dare to terminate his lease. For one thing, it might give away his intentions, for another, he might be coming back. He paid his rent for July. At that point he'd know, one way or another whether he'd still need his apartment.

He itched to read up on the rules concerning a marriage and what it took to turn it into a green card, but was too paranoid to leave a potential electronic trail. He already regretted that he'd talked about it openly on Skype. Research would have to wait until he got there. It wasn't like he'd have anything else to do.

He threw himself into work as he waited for his visa to come through, both to make it up a bit to Misha, and to keep himself from worrying too much. About what was waiting for him on the other side. What kind of man he would meet. Whether it would work out in the end. He tried not to think about returning here if it didn't. Tasha had assured him that same-sex marriage was legal where she lived, but he was pretty sure that gaming the system wasn't. And being sent back here as a criminal was . . . He could *not* go to prison in Russia. He couldn't go to prison, period.

If they tried it and failed, he'd return in a much worse position than he was in now. The possibility of prison oozed into his nightmares, though he mostly managed to banish those thoughts during daylight hours.

Of course, a thousand things could go wrong even before that. He and this Jason might take one look at each other and change their minds, or they might get to know each other and decide it was a bad idea. Hell, he might not get the fucking visa to visit the States in the first place. What was taking the embassy so long?

It wasn't the first time Arkady had been on a plane, but this was a far cry from a military transport. And it was the first time he was traveling beyond the borders of the old USSR. Because technically he might have been outside of Russia during the Second Chechen War, but he'd never really been outside its zone of influence.

The plane and personnel were German, but everyone spoke English with ease, which was a relief and made his connection in Frankfurt less stressful than he had feared. Even the uniforms were polite and friendly here.

Most of the other passengers watched a movie on the small screen in front of them during the long Atlantic crossing, but Arkady didn't get bored staring at clouds and the water below, though he was superstitiously careful not to look backward. Excitement and trepidation skittered through his veins and lungs and built in his stomach with every mile.

The attitude of the border guards in the Seattle airport was more familiar—self-important and suspicious: if you smile, it's because you're trying to hide something or because you're secretly apologizing. So Arkady kept his head down and didn't smile. He said *Yes, Sir* and *No, Sir,* and didn't fidget when he presented his passport and visa.

They waved him through to the baggage area, where he went straight into the men's restroom and threw up.

The mundane task of brushing his teeth afterward did a lot toward calming his shaking hands, and by the time he'd collected his suitcase and carried it through customs, he felt almost normal again.

They had picked him out to open his bag and suitcase, but he wasn't worried about his luggage, only about his papers. He took a deep breath when he finally stepped through to the main arrivals area. For now the worst was over.

He was scanning the crowd for Tasha's blond head when she cannonballed into his chest and wrapped her arms around his waist. Then she stood in front of him and touched his face, his arms, his hands, as if she needed to make sure that he was really here. He knew how she felt. He couldn't believe it either.

"You made it."

"I sure did." He thought the grin might split his cheeks.

She looked good. Glowing, healthy, a little tired maybe. But, then, if she'd been half as excited as he was, she wouldn't have slept much last night.

They just stood and stared at each other for a second, then Tasha's gaze became more intent when she said, "Of course my car wouldn't start this morning of all mornings, and Anna had a production meeting, so a friend from work was kind enough to give me a ride."

He winked at her to let her know he understood. *I came to visit my sister, then fell for her friend at the airport.*

"Arkady, meet Jason Cooley."

He didn't have to fake being struck. His mental image of a grizzled veteran with a cane disintegrated in light of a muscle-packed, rugged powerhouse of a man with a short beard and keen eyes that didn't seem to miss a thing.

Arkady's first thought was, *Christ, he's my age, if that.* The second one, *He's fucking hot.* Then he was done thinking.

Cooley held out his hand. "Good to finally meet you. Natalya can't stop talking about you."

That double bass voice raised goose bumps on Arkady's skin. The firm, brief handshake intensified them. Was it possible to have goose bumps on the inside of your skin? His tough-guy alert blared on every frequency. What was the protocol on fucking your potential fiancé of convenience? And why had Tasha never answered his question whether the man was gay?

Fuck, he was so, so very screwed.

CHAPTER THREE

Jason hadn't had a clear image of Arkady in mind, but from the way Natalya had been talking about him, he'd vaguely expected someone boyish. The man who shook his hand at the airport was anything but.

At first glance, the siblings had the same coloring, though the similarity ended there. Arkady was as tall as Natalya was small. Lithe and long-limbed, he stood at easy eye level with Jason's six foot two.

At second glance, his hair was a darker blond than his sister's, and where her eyes were tempered steel, his were a dreamy robin-egg blue, deep set, fringed with long, dark-blond lashes. Curved, sensual lips, and blond scruff completed the picture. A melancholy face capable of producing a blindingly sunny smile. His jacket was as old as his boots, but his luggage was new.

As a child he'd probably looked quite . . . *angelic* was the word that dusted itself off in Jason's mind. But a number of little details derailed that connotation. The decidedly chiseled jaw for one, a scar under the lower lip and one just below the cheekbone, the nose that had for sure been broken at some point. And he moved like a man who knew himself well. Jason had seen the same subconscious assurance in seasoned soldiers. Tried and not broken. Definitely a guy worth getting to know better.

He hung back to give the siblings space to talk and hug and generally get caught up on each other's lives. Not that he understood the Russian exchange anyway.

They both sat in the back of the car, Natalya with an apologetic shrug in his direction. He nodded at her. He got it. Sort of, anyway. He'd known enough people who had connections like that.

Natalya invited him inside when they got to her place and, switching to English, broke out the tequila, but they didn't linger over it. Arkady, while clearly willing, was fading fast, and Jason, of course, still had to drive home.

When he got up, Arkady did as well.

"I'm afraid, I'm going to have to crash," he said. His throaty *h* made Jason smile. "I am jet-lagged and getting drunk fast. But tomorrow night my friend Jason and I," eyes on his sister, he put an arm around Jason and lightly closed his fingers around Jason's shoulder, "are going to go to a pub. Maybe get a little drunk, maybe not."

He turned his head to look at Jason. "We need to talk. Yes?"

"I guess so." Jason was fighting not to let on how unsettling he found the sudden . . . well, not embrace, really. Buddy hug? And why was it unsettling? Because he knew Arkady was gay? Maybe. Though that didn't quite hit it.

He turned to Natalya, and Arkady didn't try to hang on. "I've got your number. I'll let you know at what time I'm off."

"Thanks." She nodded at Arkady. "We need to get you a US phone first thing in the morning. But for now, yeah, bed for you."

Friday night he texted Natalya on his way home from work to let her know he could meet Arkady at the Gull in an hour. That gave him time for a quick shower and to change out of his uniform. Part of changing his clothes was habit—old rules of not wearing utilities off base—but he also plain hated the fact that everyone and their grandmother seemed to have a need to talk to him when he was wearing a uniform. Any uniform. It was the weirdest thing. The security company he worked for was a private one, but the uniform seemed to make him public property in people's eyes. Made his skin crawl.

The days were warm enough, but the nights could get chilly, so he went with jeans and a T-shirt, and threw an old canvas jacket over that. Plus it gave him a place to stick his keys and wallet.

He walked over, as always consciously striving for a natural gait. It didn't take as much concentration as it used to, but he doubted walking would ever feel as natural again as it was supposed to.

He was early and the first one to arrive. Business was practically nonexistent: one guy at the bar, a couple of out-of-place tourists at one of the tables on the right. Jason picked a table on the left.

Eventually the goal would be to be seen together, maybe. But for now he only wanted to test the waters. If things worked out, they'd have to meet at more popular, more public places than this little hole-in-the-wall. But as long as they were laying out the parameters of what would basically mean screwing over immigration, he was just dandy with a tad more privacy. The mission was to find out as much as he could about what kind of man Arkady was. So he'd watch and listen. Most guys loved to talk about themselves. In fact, letting them talk wasn't as much the problem as getting them to shut up again at some point. He was good at listening and making people talk to him.

Arkady showed up ten minutes later. Tan chinos and a black T-shirt. Classy. Natalya must not have briefed him about the nature of the dive they were meeting in. He was clean-shaven and smelled faintly of cigarettes when he bent down to shake Jason's hand.

He leaned in so close, that for a second Jason was sure Arkady was going to kiss him. Maybe it was a Russian thing. Different ideas about personal space.

But Arkady merely asked, "So, what does a guy typically drink around here?"

Jason shrugged. "Beer." He nodded at the bar. "Only one on tap. You go get it, pay for it, and find a seat or stay at the bar."

Arkady frowned. "You want me to stay at the bar?"

"No. Typically. Why would I want you to stay at the bar?"

Now it was Arkady's turn to shrug. He half straightened, but then seemed to change his mind. He pushed his chin out. "Because I'm gay?"

Jason laughed. "Getting things out of the way early, are we?" He ticked it off on his thumb and index. "One: I don't want you to stay at the bar. Two: you being gay does not stop me from drinking with you. So, save yourself the attitude, go get yourself a beer, and sit your gay ass down in that chair."

He pointed at the chair for emphasis.

Arkady nodded. "Point taken." He half turned, then looked back. "I take it you're not, then?"

"What, gay? No, I'm not. Does that change your plans?"

"No. In fact, it's probably easier that way." Then he finally turned and went over to the bar.

Jason watched him, because he didn't have anything better to do. He felt a little like he'd been caught with his hand in the cookie jar, because there was some weird knot in his insides that he didn't like. But it was definitely not about objecting to having a beer with the man. So that was a relief. At least he didn't totally fail at humanity.

But still. Something about Arkady threw him off-kilter, and that bugged him. Because he couldn't figure out what or why.

When Arkady came back, he set his glass on the table and installed himself on the rickety chair, leaning back and stretching his legs out, until Jason thought the chair would split under the strain.

Arkady folded his arms across his chest. Not a good sign. He was still on the defensive, then. Not that Jason was surprised. From what Natalya had told him, Arkady hadn't exactly lived a charmed life in Russia. He was probably more used to wary alertness than peace and comfort.

Jason raised his glass. "Fuck homophobia," he said deliberately.

Arkady raised one eyebrow, then he laughed and mirrored the gesture. "I'll gladly drink to that."

They were silent for a minute, then Jason said softly, "Tell me about yourself. Who is Arkady Izmaylov?"

"Arkady Nikolayevich Izmaylov." That seemed important to him. But after that quick rejoinder, he stalled, then shrugged. "Not much to tell. Born not quite thirty years ago in a town between Moscow and Petersburg you've likely never heard of. Studied, then taught Russian and English lit at Petersburg U, until they fired me because I'm gay." He paused and stared into his beer.

A lit prof? That was a surprise. "Natalya said you worked as an electrician."

"Yeah, my cousin has an installation and repair shop. I worked there now and then as a kid and as a student. When I got laid off, he offered me a job. He's a good guy, Misha."

Jason didn't comment, just kept looking expectantly over the rim of his glass as he took a sip, watching Arkady's eyes slowly crinkle at the corners as he gave back stare for stare. Then a smile tugged at the corners of Arkady's mouth and grew into an I-know-what-you're-doing grin. "Let me guess," he said. "That wasn't enough. What do you want to hear?"

So much for it being easy to make other men talk. Jason kept his expression carefully blank. Bad enough that his game had been recognized and called. He didn't need Arkady to know that that grin was rattling him. Especially since he didn't know why.

They were having a little pissing contest. What of it? He'd been having those since he could walk, and he'd been called on them a million times. There was nothing sharkish or threatening about the man's grin. If anything, it was good-natured. It said, *I don't mind.* There was zero reason to be rattled. "What do you want to tell me?"

Again that quick grin, but then Arkady grew serious. "Fair enough. I am asking rather a lot of you."

Jason had to stop himself from protesting that no, Arkady wasn't asking that much, because he was. He was asking Jason to marry him. Only on paper, but it wasn't quite that easy if they wanted to get away with it. They would have to make it believable. The more Jason knew about the Russian, the better. For both of them.

Arkady was staring over Jason's shoulder, maybe at the window, though his thoughts seemed to be far away. "We used to go to the dacha every summer when I was a kid." He looked at Jason. "You know, like a cottage? Summer house?" He laughed. "Don't get any grand ideas, though. We aren't talking much better than a wooden shack here: no running water, no electricity. My parents, Tasha and me, our cousin Misha and his parents—his dad and mine are brothers. Two rooms. The girls would get the bedroom, and us guys would take the great room. My uncle always got the sofa, because he's the oldest. The rest of us slept on the floor. We'd bring cans and some bread, and otherwise fished and hunted for meat. We'd hunt rabbits with our bare hands, Tasha and I. Just for the hell of it. Never expected to catch one. Only, I did once, and didn't know what to do next. Soft little thing, heart beating like a drum against my hands. I think I was as terrified as the rabbit. Scratched me up pretty bad until

Tasha took it from me and broke its neck. Then she threw up in the bushes. We delivered it to my mother for the table and never talked about it again." After all those years he still looked a bit green around the gills at the memory.

He emptied his glass and went to get a new one. He came back with a beer for Jason as well. "What about you?"

Jason had expected the question, had thought about what to say. "Military family. Both of my parents were soldiers."

"Were?"

"My father still is. My mother is dead. I was raised by my grandparents. Grandpa had already been a soldier. Korea. I signed up out of high school. Served a couple of years, got blown up and sent home, got a job." He said it the same way Arkady had said he'd been fired for being gay. No big deal. Not much of a story. The way honest men tell lies.

"Your parents were in the Gulf?"

Jason nodded, then gave Arkady a level stare. "And Afghanistan."

Arkady threw up both hands in a gesture of peace. "Hey, I'm too young to have been in Afghanistan. Or are you afraid this is a my-parents-fought-against-your-parents thing? I doubt it. No career soldiers in my family. All strictly conscripts." He showed his teeth, then studied his knuckles. "For what it's worth, I don't think either of our countries deserves a medal for that war." He looked at Jason from under his brows, a hard-to-read stare. Challenge? Defensive? Whatever, Jason didn't feel like talking about either the US or his own involvement in any war.

Before he'd decided on an answer, Arkady leaned toward him and said quietly, "Listen. I'm not planning to make your life difficult or take up a lot of space. All I need is a piece of paper. We draw up the application, and you'll never have to see me again."

Seriously? Jason felt his eyebrow shoot up. "Half-assed planning, Izmaylov." He also leaned forward. Like two dogs in a pit. But their hands were almost touching.

And why was he noticing that?

"They check that shit. You can't afford to be sent back to Russia, and I can't afford to go to jail. So, we'll do this properly or not at all."

At the mention of jail, Arkady tilted his head to the side, speculation and open curiosity warring in his face. "Why exactly *are* you doing this?"

Jason leaned back. "I need the money."

"You haven't mentioned the money. Not once."

"Why would I? I hadn't said yes yet."

"And now you have?" Arkady's eyes had grown intent, and he was leaning forward even more, as if he were trying to follow Jason, stay on his heels.

It gave Jason pause. Had he just said yes? Was he being a fool? He still had so many questions, and not a few doubts. But what choice did he have, really? He did need the money. Only it wasn't that. Getting people out of tight spots was what he did, who he was. The only thing he'd ever been good at. There was no way he'd send Arkady packing, back to Russia where homosexuals were hunted like rats.

He'd never left anyone behind. Couldn't if he tried. He knew *left behind*; it was etched into his DNA. No way could he do that to someone else. He'd paid half a leg for that inability already. He briefly wondered what it would cost him now.

Arkady hadn't moved a muscle. He was gripping the edge of the table hard enough for his knuckles to turn white.

Jason gave himself another heartbeat to reconsider, to abort the mission. Then he said, "I guess I have."

The pavement still reflected the heat of the day when they left the pub, but a breeze from the ocean promised a cool night ahead. Jason shoved both hands into his jacket pockets. He turned to Arkady to make a remark about it looking like rain, but swallowed it when he noticed the Russian squaring his shoulders.

He instinctively followed Arkady's gaze to a group of five men about to cross the road in their direction. Had they been spotted? And why the hell was he even asking himself that? Apparently Arkady's skittishness was contagious. Wait, was that Tommy Hawkins? He knew those guys. Two of them worked security on set; they talked too much, gossiped even, but harmless stuff. Gossips, though . . . he could use that. Since he'd made up his mind to fake a relationship, the time to spread the word was now.

He quickly scanned the area, then pulled Arkady into the doorway behind them—out of the way enough to make it seem like he was trying for privacy, but perfectly visible under the porch light. With any luck, this would look intimate enough from across the road, and if he knew his colleagues well, by Monday it would be all over the studio that they were a couple.

Bracing himself with one arm against the doorjamb, he slipped the other hand around Arkady's neck and bent his head to whisper, "Just play along for a minute," against Arkady's ear.

Arkady was standing with his back to the door, but even so, Jason felt his recoil. He was about to straighten up and apologize, when Arkady suddenly relaxed, then pulled Jason against him in a bear hug and kissed him full on the lips.

What the— Jason's brain mirrored Arkady's recoil, but that recoil never made it into action. Apparently his body had completely different ideas about that kiss. Like kissing back, for one. Like pressing into Arkady's body. Like shutting down Jason's brain and pumping the blood to where it was really needed.

The cool breeze raised the little hairs on Jason's neck. Or maybe that was Arkady's hand moving up under Jason's shirt, fingertips skittering along his spine, leaving a trail of fire.

There was no movement except forward, no time but now, and no room for thought outside of that single-minded pursuit of Arkady's lips. Jason tried to make out taste or texture, but lost himself in a barrage of sensations. His hand, loosely curled against Arkady's throat, picked up a rumble that hummed up against his lips in a low moan.

He barely registered the wolf whistle behind him, but Arkady's body instantly turned to stone.

Jason turned, trying to suppress the snarl, trying to kick his brain into gear. The chorus of whistles, jeers, and recommendations to get a room didn't sound aggressive, though. Tommy Hawkins and friends merely couldn't keep from commenting as they moved past. A last lewd gesture, then they were gone, the door of the pub swinging closed behind them.

Arkady's eyes shone like silver under the lamplight, hands pressed against the door like he was ready to fling himself forward. Whether for fight or flight, Jason had no idea.

"Shhh . . ." Jason said softly, and laid a calming hand against Arkady's chest. Heartbeat like thunder against his palm. "Relax. It's fine."

"*Pizdets.*"

Jason raised his hands in an international I-don't-understand gesture. "I'm sorry, I . . ."

But Arkady didn't elaborate, and his voice had been so inflectionless that he could have said anything. *I'm okay*, or *Shit*, or *You bastard.*

"I'm really sorry," Jason said again. "I was only going to pretend. I never meant to . . ." What? *Kiss you? Scare you?* He shook his head. "Let's get out of here."

But Arkady didn't move. "What the fucking fuck was that?" he hissed.

Instant boom, a voice in Jason's brain provided gleefully. Which wasn't an answer.

What the fuck *had* just happened?

Boom.

Shut up.

He had to admit that he felt a bit shaken. But if there had been any boom, it had been the surprise of meeting another man's lips. Surely.

You didn't stop at the lips.

Whatever. He didn't have time to dwell on that now. He had a mission to plan, and he knew from long practice and experience how to push any unrelated thoughts to the back of his mind for now.

Arkady hadn't moved a muscle, was very obviously still waiting for an answer. Jason nodded toward the pub. "Guys I work with. If we want news of us having hooked up to spread as fast as possible, to give our story some credibility, that was probably the quickest way to do it. By tomorrow evening, it'll be the newest studio gossip."

Arkady's unrelenting stare was making him fidgety. And defensive. So, maybe he *was* avoiding the issue here, but he didn't have an answer for that, did he? He shrugged. "Hey, I saw an opportunity and took it. I'm sorry about the misunderstanding. That kiss took me as much by surprise as it did you. Can we move on now? As I see it, you come home with me—you can have the couch—and we make a big production of entering and leaving the house together, hoping one of the neighbors will see us."

Arkady frowned. "Are you saying that immigration, or whoever, is going to ask your neighbors about us?"

"Friends, family, neighbors. Don't you watch any movies?"

"Not the right ones, apparently."

Jason felt himself blush, but he wasn't going to apologize for watching chick flicks. That was nobody's business but his own.

"And you're telling me you're okay with that . . . gossip?" There was still a wired tension in Arkady's shoulders, but he was slowly starting to sound more like himself.

"If I wasn't, why the fuck would I have agreed with your plan? Your sister's plan. Whatever."

Arkady shrugged, but didn't answer. He still seemed on guard. At least he was finally coming out of his shock freeze.

"Well, do you have a better plan?"

Arkady shook his head, then pushed himself off the door. "Lead the way, then."

CHAPTER FOUR

The wind carried that particular blend of briny and clean scent one only got from the ocean. Arkady sucked it deeply into his lungs and waited for the jitters to subside.

He knew how to deal with the adrenaline rush of being cornered, that hot apprehension of getting hurt, maybe killed. And he knew how to ride that other rush, the one that came with roaming hands and spicy kisses. But getting blindsided by both at the same time had rocked him harder than he cared for. He threw a glance at Jason's profile, a sharp contrast of deep shadow and the actinic glare of the streetlight.

He couldn't believe he was going home with a stranger. Had the circumstances been the least bit different, he would have told Jason to stuff it. Thoughts flew like sparks, trying to light a fire Arkady didn't want lit. His brain could barely keep up with worrying about everything worth worrying over. Like, what kind of man married another man for money, if he wasn't even gay? Maybe Tasha was right, and it didn't really matter; the circumstances were what they were. Truth was, Arkady couldn't afford to piss Jason off for nothing. Not unless he wanted to call the whole thing off. That was the only reason he'd agreed to come along now; the kiss had nothing to do with that. He needed Jason, but he didn't have to trust him, or like him. No matter how hot he was. Or how likable.

Fuck it, straight guys were not supposed to kiss like that. Not other guys anyway. And they were sure as hell not supposed to be that unconcerned about being kissed by mistake. There'd been no outrage from Jason, no posturing, just a mild surprise. As if their lips had met fleetingly by an accident quickly corrected, when it had been nothing of the sort.

Jason had answered that kiss as if he'd meant it, had gotten lips, tongue, teeth, and hands involved in that kiss that had rocked Arkady to the bottom of his boots. What if they hadn't been interrupted by Jason's buddies? What then?

They walked in complete silence until Jason stopped in front of a small house with an ancient Toyota Camry sitting in front of the garage. He made a sweeping gesture at the somewhat overgrown front yard. "This is me."

Arkady wasn't sure what he'd expected, but this wasn't it. He needed to get used to America catching him by surprise. Apparently single men in their twenties owned their own houses in this country.

He became suddenly aware of Jason watching him, and shrugged his musings off. "Is this where you invite me in for a drink?" he asked deadpan.

Jason grinned. "You read my mind. Do you want to come in for a drink?" He gave Arkady a conspiratorial wink that sent a rush of heat through Arkady's body.

Fuck, he wanted to kiss this guy again. Jesus, fuck, he needed to get a grip. Fast. No matter how well Jason had dealt with that accidental kiss, there'd be a limit to his tolerance. And Arkady really didn't want to get on the bad side of a guy who looked like he could throw him all the way back to Russia with one hand tied behind his back. He lowered his head, as much in assent as to hide his face from those perceptive eyes. "I thought you'd never ask."

After unlocking the front door, Jason flicked a switch on the inside, silhouetting the two of them in the wide-open doorway for long moment, before reaching around Arkady and pulling the door closed behind him. All part of the grand plan, presumably.

The hallway was short and very tight, especially with someone of Jason's bulk taking up most of the space and emanating the kind of body heat Arkady could feel through his shirt. Not making eye contact seemed like a seriously good idea right now, so he ended up studying the broken orange and brown linoleum under his feet. There was a tinkle of keys and then finally breathing room.

"Are you coming?" Jason asked over his shoulder.

Arkady followed him into a large room with a rough wood floor. A line down the middle indicated where a wall had been torn out. The remaining walls needed painting. A couch, armchair, low table, and TV unit with a large flat-screen TV were the only furniture. All relatively new, solid, no frills. The curtains covering the windows were the exact opposite: Clean, but yellow with age and decidedly frilly.

"This your parents' house?"

"Grandparents.'"

Suddenly the whole jumbled look made sense.

"You're renovating."

"I was. Started when I first got back from rehab. Mostly because I was bored to tears and in danger of self-pity."

That last one didn't seem likely for the man Arkady was slowly getting to know. He was about to say so, when Jason continued. "I guess I was trying to, I dunno, make it my own? Make it a place where I . . ." He stalled, took a breath as if to start again, then shrugged. "Anyway, I got a job, needed more money, picked up more shifts." He indicated the wall behind him, the upper half of which had been taken out, creating a large opening into the kitchen. A board provided a sort of breakfast bar between the two rooms, but the sides and top needed finishing. "Not worth it."

Not worth what? Finishing? Worrying about finishing? Arkady followed him into the kitchen. "What do you need the money for? You don't seem to lead an expensive life." It felt rude, asking that, but he really needed to know.

Jason tapped a photograph of a toddler with pigtails and dimples that had been tacked to the fridge door with a magnet. "This is Lily, my daughter. I'm working on her college fund. Now it turns out she's gifted and needs to go to a special school too." It was said with a comical mix of pride and desperation, but Arkady didn't think it was funny to Jason.

"You're married, then? Divorced?"

Jason shook his head. "We were never married, Lily's mom and I." He stared into space, maybe at a memory.

Something, a certain wistfulness in his expression, made Arkady ask, "Is she the one that got away? Her mom?"

A half smile flickered across Jason's face that was downright painful to watch. "Maybe. She made me feel like I belonged somewhere." Then he shook himself. "Water under the bridge. She's happily married now to one of the nicest guys I know."

Just like with the kiss earlier, there was no anger, no resentment in his voice. He seemed to be graced with infinite patience and capacity for understanding.

Suddenly Arkady felt a lot better about Tasha's crazy plan of importing him into a foreign country and marrying him to a stranger. "You are so not like Russian men."

A little crease appeared between Jason's brows. "Sorry?"

"No, don't be. I like it. It's very relaxing."

He got a doubtful look, but Jason didn't pursue the matter. "Do you want a beer?" he asked instead, opening the fridge without waiting for a reply.

"Sure."

Beer took up the whole bottom shelf of the fridge. The rest was scantily stocked with bread, mayo, cheese, ham, and half a head of lettuce. Arkady recognized sandwich territory when he saw it.

Jason apparently followed his train of thought and grinned. "I suck at cooking. You?"

"I'm the king of instant noodles," Arkady offered.

Jason laughed. "Great. We're fucked."

They took their beers over to the sofa, where Jason sat with one knee up facing Arkady. "We need to talk this through. Have a solid plan that puts us on the same page when we're asked."

"About what exactly?"

"Feelings, romance, crap like that."

"A staunch believer in romance, are you?"

Jason huffed.

It wasn't crap, though. And the completely unreasonable desire to show Jason, prove to him that romance wasn't crap was strong. Jet lag probably. He was such a mess.

Good thing that Jason at least was about as excitable as a rock. One of them needed to keep a cool head.

With an exaggerated gesture, Arkady pointed at himself. "Well, I'm hopelessly romantic. Want to lay out your grand plan for me?

I might be able to embellish the details." *When you can't win, laugh about yourself.*

"Okay. Here it is. Operation Green Card. Listen closely."

"Should we write this down?" Arkady was having a hard time switching back to serious mode.

But apparently Jason didn't notice. "No. If we do get a visit from immigration, I don't want to have to worry about every scrap of paper ever written in this house. Except in here," He moved his index finger back and forth between his and Arkady's head. "We're a couple. The story is: instant chemistry."

Arkady swallowed but didn't interrupt. There was nothing he could have said, anyway, but he sure wouldn't have to lie about the instant-chemistry thing.

"The story is: we start seeing each other, we fall in love, we marry." Jason's finger tapped the table on every one of those points. "Maybe we marry a bit faster than we would've done if your visa didn't run out, but that's all there's to it; nothing to see here, moving on." His eyes were intense, focused. "Think of it as an acting role you have to play pretty much 24/7. The more you live the story, the less likely you are to be caught in a lie."

Arkady leaned back. "You sound like an undercover cop."

That drew a laugh from Jason. "Close. Airborne Pathfinders, personnel recovery. Flying under the radar was a good way to stay alive."

"Personnel recovery. As in extracting soldiers from behind enemy lines?"

Jason nodded, then pointed his bottle at the window. "Wonder if I should take the curtains down to give the neighbors a better view. Never liked them anyway. The curtains. The neighbors are decent."

Arkady blinked at the sudden change in topic. "Er, you want to bring your acting ambitions indoors as well?"

"Yeah, that might be a bit more than we can handle."

Clearly the topic of Jason's military career was closed, but Arkady didn't feel like letting it go. He needed to know this man, partly for the pretense, partly for his own safety. And then there was that niggling little voice that just wanted to see how far Jason could be pushed. Nobody could be that cool forever, could they?

"Is that how you lost your leg? During personnel recovery?"

Jason gaped at him with such shock and misery on his face that Arkady was almost sorry he'd asked.

"How'd— Am I—" With a visible effort, Jason collected himself and took a swig of beer. He nearly choked on it, then let out a rush of air in what sounded like a desperate attempt at laughter. He leaned back into his couch corner and stretched the fingers of his free hand. *Trying to relax*, Arkady thought.

"I guess I was hoping it wouldn't be that obvious," Jason finally said. "What gave me away?"

"Nothing. Tasha told me."

"And how did she— Oh. When she barged in on me in front of Krueger's office? I think he mentioned it?"

"I have no idea. I assumed it was common knowledge." It would take some serious determination to hide a missing leg from people who saw him every day.

"No." The little sun marks in the corners of Jason's eyes tightened. "It isn't. And I'd like to keep it that way."

Yup, determination, all right. Even if his uniform presumably didn't include shorts. Arkady decided he'd pushed far enough for one night, nodded, and kept his mouth shut. He was doing a lot of that lately.

After a minute of silence, Jason continued on his own. "It was a recovery mission that didn't go according to plan. We completed the mission." He paused, then said with emphasis, "I've never not completed a mission."

Arkady wasn't sure if that was a general point of pride, or meant to reassure him as far as Operation Green Card was concerned.

"But the price for that one was way higher than I'd bargained for. I should've insisted on g—" His gaze, which had been far away, focused abruptly and he shrugged. "So yeah . . ."

"I would never have known if Tasha hadn't mentioned it," Arkady said, trying to make up for kicking a now-obvious sore spot.

He didn't get an answer. So much for trying to make the guy feel better. Time to get back to the original topic.

"So, the plan is what? Have some public dates?" What he really wanted to ask was whether that would involve any more public kissing, but it hadn't been Jason who'd started that, had it? Next time Arkady would know better where to draw the pretend line. *Acting, my ass.* Well, he'd better brush up on techniques for stage kisses.

"Yeah," Jason said. "Spend some time together. Make it look like we're hitting it off."

"Romantic walks on the beach?" Jason rolled his eyes, which made Arkady laugh. "Hey, you're the one who suggested we live the role. Your romantic streak needs some polishing. What better practice?"

His answer was an exasperated stare, then Jason stretched and got up. "You keep thinking up those romantic schemes. I need to go to bed. Alarm rings at 4 a.m." He pointed at the couch. "It pulls out. Bed stuff's in the box. Bathroom's upstairs; use whatever you need. Towels in the linen closet on the landing. Any questions?"

Arkady had a quip about room service on the tip of his tongue, but swallowed it. Things were complicated enough for now, and Jason did look tired.

"I'm good. Go, get some sleep. I'll see you in the morning."

After Jason had gone upstairs, Arkady busied himself with making his bed, listening to the sounds of steps upstairs, creaking doors and running water, until there was nothing but silence. He slipped under the blankets, but he wasn't the least bit sleepy. Definitely jet-lagged. He was also alone and curious. Fuck courtesy—this might be the best opportunity he'd get to find out a little more about Jason Cooley. He got up and started opening cabinets, beginning with the one under the TV. Two shelves packed with DVDs were meticulously sorted into fitness videos, documentaries, movies. Half of them Arkady had never heard of, but he recognized the titles of certain action movies and . . . rom-coms. "I'll be damned." Arkady pulled out a copy of *Moonstruck* and looked up the stairs with a grin tugging at the corners of his mouth. "Not the romantic kind, huh? You big fat liar, you're so busted."

He didn't find any books, just a handful of hunting magazines. Only one small drawer of CDs: some metal, some pop—Dido, Beyoncé, Jewel, one hard-rock Christmas mix. Not exactly an extensive collection, but then the guy didn't spend much time away from work. He probably had music on his phone. Unless he didn't listen to music. Was that even a thing?

The kitchen cabinets were equally bare. Apart from scant cleaning paraphernalia under the sink, the cabinets harbored protein powder, a half-empty box of Cap'n Crunch, assorted dishes, a bag of oatmeal, and cutlery and gadgets in a couple of drawers.

Arkady stood in the middle of the kitchen, nonplussed and slightly sad at the lack of anything that revealed passion, or joy, or personal connections. His gaze strayed to the door of the fridge and got stuck on the picture of the little girl. Except for that. She had Jason's eyes, and his clear, penetrating gaze. Arkady hadn't found any toys, but she most likely had a room upstairs for when she came to visit. A weekend-a-month arrangement? Jason had sounded like he was on good terms with his ex, so it seemed likely.

Since he was already prowling, Arkady decided to have a look at the basement as well. The main room held a very decent gym, a washer/dryer combo, a shelf with tools next to the water heater. A door in the back led to the furnace. Everything tidy and reasonably clean. No secrets, no skeletons. If there was anything worthwhile left to be discovered about Cooley, it was either upstairs or nothing tangible.

He woke to the soft gurgle of the coffee maker and the smell of fresh brew. The world beyond the windows was still pitch-black, the kitchen only illuminated by a weak light above the stove.

Jason moved around the kitchen as silently as a ghost. From his position on the couch, Arkady only saw Jason's head and shoulders above the breakfast bar. Bare, powerful shoulders that flexed and relaxed hypnotically as Jason ghosted to the fridge. He was briefly outlined against its light, then the fridge door closed with a soft *thwack*, and Arkady shook himself out of his trance. Jason's movements suggested crutches, but how did that not make a noise?

But then Jason crossed from the kitchen to the hallway, and Arkady realized that he'd used the counters like crutches, just as he was now using the banisters on either side of the stairs. And the things that was doing to his shoulder and back muscles left Arkady's mouth dry. The fact that he was wearing nothing but a pair of black boxer briefs didn't help. Jason disappeared upstairs out of his line of sight before Arkady registered that he hadn't been wearing a prosthesis, and that his left leg ended below the knee. The sound of a shower trickled down the stairs, and Arkady sat up. The glowing digits of a clock under the TV read 04:14. *You've got to be fucking kidding me.*

With a groan he sank back down on his pillow, but the more he tried to ignore the susurration of running water, the more his bladder screamed for relief.

The water stopped. Arkady sat up and pulled on his T-shirt. He waited for the clacking of the doors, bathroom, bedroom, before racing up the steps two at a time.

The soft *click* of the door to his left on the upper landing barely registered in his brain before he barreled into a still water-beaded, hard chest. Jason's hand shot out to the banister to steady himself, the other arm closed around Arkady to keep him from sprawling back down the stairs. Body heat, the smell of soap, two heartbeats thudding chest to chest. And a pair of hazel eyes so close that they were slightly out of focus. Noses almost touching, lips . . .

Jason let him go and gave him space. Droplets ran down the poster child of a six-pack and into the top of a towel slung around a solid ass and hips. "Sorry. Didn't mean to wake you," Jason rumbled. His voice almost an octave deeper than normal.

"I need to—" Arkady started at the same time as Jason said, "Forgot my—"

They both stopped, then Jason gestured at the bathroom door. "Go ahead."

With the closed door between them, Arkady was able to breathe again. He had to lean nearly horizontally over the toilet in order to relieve himself. *Christ.* He tried to remember if Jason had looked down, because that boner would have been embarrassingly obvious covered by nothing but briefs and a T-shirt. He was making a complete and utter fool of himself over a straight guy. A straight guy he was going to marry. Who insisted on pretending they were falling for each other. Arkady almost laughed. Was Jason ever in for a surprise at how well Arkady could act.

He washed his hands and caught his own eyes in the mirror. *Fuck.* He was fucked. He spared a fond thought for the grizzled, shot-up vet image he'd had of Jason when Tasha had first told him of her plan, then braced himself to face his downfall.

But when he opened the door, there was no sign of Jason.

He went back to the living room to get dressed and fold up his bed things back into the couch.

This time when Jason came downstairs, he was in a dark-gray uniform with a company logo on the shoulder and his name tag on his chest. Nothing in his gait even hinted at the fact that he was missing a leg. He swept one of his penetrating gazes across Arkady and the neatly made-up couch, then went into the kitchen. "There's coffee if you want. Me, I can't eat this early, but you're welcome to whatever I have."

Arkady swallowed the decidedly lewd request that immediately jumped to the forefront of his mind. He leaned on the breakfast bar and watched Jason make a pile of sandwiches that would easily have fed a class of third graders.

When he'd finally wrangled his mind under control, Arkady said, "I'll take the coffee, thanks."

When he took the mug of black brew from Jason, he made damned sure their hands didn't touch. Just thinking about that gave him a jolt he didn't need.

Absolutely nothing had happened last night, nor would it, ever. Then, why did this feel like the world's supremely awkward morning after I-should-have-left-last-night?

He sipped his coffee, casting around for a safe topic to fill the silence, when his shirt caught on the rough edge of the bar top. "So, have you given up on your renovations?"

"No. I don't know." Jason huffed a laugh. "Most nights I'm too exhausted to notice, but every time I have a minute, I hate it. I like things neat, not this unfinished crap." His hand wave seemed to include the whole house plus the land it stood on, plus unseen *things* he couldn't or maybe didn't want to find words for. He sighed. "But is it worth it? At some point I'll have to decide how likely I am to finish. Might be better to sell this place as a fixer-upper and move on."

"No emotional attachment, happy memories?"

"No."

Arkady winced at the bleakness of that, and Jason seemed to have noticed, because he shrugged. "No particularly bad ones, either. It's the house I grew up in. That's it. The only thing keeping me here right now is that it's cheap. Though at the rate those Hollywood people are driving up the property taxes, that might not be for long."

It was said matter-of-factly enough that Arkady thought the loss he read between the lines might be his own rather than Jason's. Yet, against his better judgment, he felt compelled to offer something, some comfort, some solution.

"I have nothing to do except play tourist here," he heard himself say. "And I'm not unhandy. If you tell me what you want done and trust me with your keys, I'd be perfectly willing to lend a hand."

Jason's gaze grew speculative. "Why would you want to do that?"

Taking his heart in both hands Arkady said with a straight face, "Because I've had the fiercest crush on you ever since we first met." Then he screwed up his face into a classic cartoon wink. It worked. Jason burst out laughing.

"Good one. And a good idea, too, about the keys. There's a spare one hanging right by the door. About the reno though? Waste of time." He checked his watch. "How about I take you back to your sister's now and let you work your romance genius on something nice for tonight?" He tried to copy the cartoon wink, but broke up laughing again. "Text me when you've got something?"

"I will. I might even put on something pretty." The earlier tension between them was gone, and for the first time, Arkady thought that this whole thing might actually work.

CHAPTER FIVE

Jason dropped Arkady off at Natalya's place and watched until the door closed behind him, then tried to call himself to order. But this whole not-thinking-about-the-kiss-because-he-had-a-mission-to-plan thing wasn't working. Not with Arkady bumping into him half-naked at odd hours, and weird sparks flying between them. Or maybe that was just him. Which didn't really help, because he couldn't figure out why it was happening. Despite having been jerked off and sucked off by other guys, and despite occasionally admiring male beauty, he wasn't gay. He didn't think he was, anyway. He liked women and sex with women. And he'd certainly never dreamed of being in a relationship with a man. Hell, he'd never even wanted to kiss one. Until yesterday. He felt a little betrayed by the fact that kissing Arkady had been quite so . . . arousing. He was aware of the man in ways he wasn't usually aware of male bodies.

That didn't change over the next couple of days, the next couple of meetings. Otherwise why would he notice Arkady licking beer foam off his lip, or how his throat moved when he swallowed, or how the oil ran down his long fingers when he bit into a slice of pizza?

And it didn't change when Arkady brought over his suitcase and a box of books, when he unpacked his toothbrush, and when he showed up for coffee the next morning with a bit of shaving foam stuck to the edge of his jaw. The urge to wipe it off, to run his thumb along that edge and across those full lips was so strong that Jason had to turn away. He rinsed out his coffee mug to the pounding of his heart in his throat.

It didn't bother him that he might be gay, but it bugged the hell out of him that he didn't know if he was. Shouldn't a grown man know these things about himself?

He picked up Mark, and they sat in their usual silence in the car, Mark checking and answering emails like he always did. Jason couldn't help throwing sideways glances at him, trying to decide whether he could ask him some stuff. Mark was a nice guy, and Jason trusted him. Definitely not one of the gossip squad, Mark. But he might not appreciate getting personal questions just because he happened to be the only openly gay man Jason knew.

Suddenly Mark looked up. "Yeees?"

"I didn't say anything," Jason growled.

"Not yet. Are you going to say something, or were you merely admiring my looks?"

Shit. He didn't think he'd been that obvious about it.

"I need to ask something. But you can ignore me. It's kinda private."

"Yeees?" It sounded a little more wary this time, but not like a shutdown.

"Have you ever kissed a girl?" Jason asked before he could chicken out.

"No."

"Huh."

The silences between them were never uncomfortable, but not exactly communicative either. Drumming his fingers on the wheel at the one red light between Bluewater Bay and the studio, Jason asked, "Did you ever want to?"

"No."

"Not even curious?"

"Not really."

Jason was keeping his eyes on the road, but could feel Mark watching him. He'd ask what this was about any second now, and Jason wasn't sure how to answer that.

"When did you know you were gay?" Jason asked and threw a glance to his right. Mark's eyebrow shot up, and Jason knew immediately that that had somehow been the wrong question.

"When did you know you were straight?" Mark shot back, his voice very cool now.

Jason grunted. He owed Mark an answer, didn't he? "That's just it. I don't think I do know."

"Let me guess, you're afraid something or someone turned you gay?"

That was a weirdly aggressive way of putting it. It sounded as if Mark had heard it before, and more than once. And he was tense, almost defensive, as if he expected an attack. Jason decided he needed to explain some more, clear the air. "I don't believe you can turn someone gay, and it wouldn't bother me if I was. What bothers me is that I can't figure this out. I'm not twelve anymore. I should know this."

Next to him Mark relaxed, but didn't offer any advice. So Jason stumbled on.

"I've always liked women. Still do, in fact. So why—" He took a deep breath. "I met a guy recently who pushes buttons I didn't know I had."

"Buttons as in sex?"

Jason shook his head. "Worse. Kissing."

Mark laughed out loud. "That's worse? How?"

Fuck. He didn't want to think about an answer to that question, but pitching Mark into the ditch just so he wouldn't have to was probably not good strategy, was it? Really, he should be happy Mark was making an effort to figure this out with him, but goddamn it, this was awkward.

"It's more . . . intimate somehow. Involved. I dunno."

"More intimate than what?"

Jason shrugged. "Jerking each other off, getting blown? Those are just about getting off. No names, no talk, no acknowledgment that it happened. You know?"

Mark nodded slowly. "Yeah, I think I know what you mean. Still, looks to me like you've always swung both ways a bit?"

"Huh?"

Mark sighed. "Have you ever considered you might be bisexual?"

"Oh, come on."

"What?"

"Isn't that just a fancier term for 'hasn't figured it out yet'?"

Mark opened his mouth, then closed it and sighed. "You know what? Google it."

Jason had put his foot in it again, then? "Sorry, didn't mean any offense."

"No, I know." Mark pinched his eyebrows. "This . . . It gets really old at some point. Also, we're here. So, do us both a favor, google it, at least skim the Wikipedia article, do some research, and if you still want to talk after that, I'll be here, okay?"

"Okay, thanks."

He parked the car, and they started walking in different directions to their respective work areas, when Mark turned back to him and said, "Good kissers are keepers, by the way." Then he left.

Great. Like that was an option.

He climbed up to the surveillance center, careful, as always, not to show a limp or to stumble.

Pete, who'd been on nightshift, technically had another thirty minutes, but he signed out the second Jason stepped into the room and whizzed past with a quick "All clear." Likely trying to make it home in time to cook breakfast for his son and take him to the school bus, then crash. Jason briefly wondered when Lily would have to be on the school bus and what she'd have for breakfast. Useless random thoughts—they just popped up sometimes.

He glanced at Pete's one-page report. All clear, indeed. There'd been no filming going on that night; the whole shift must've been boring as hell.

He settled in front of the monitors, and watched the day start and familiar faces pass the gates. *"Have you ever considered you might be bisexual?"*

So this was actually a thing? For real? But the more he tried to scoff at it, the more it settled around his shoulders like it might fit.

At nine thirty, he dug out his thermos and sandwiches and typed *bisexual* into his phone. Sharing his attention with one more screen didn't seem like a big deal, but it was harder than he'd thought not to get lost in reading, and the first tour group was coming through. That kid down there was doing his best to get himself lost. Jason grabbed the receiver and pressed the button for the main gate house. "You have a family of five coming through," he said when Turner picked up. "Black and orange stroller. Their toddler—Spiderman hoodie—just peeled off to the left. Grab him and head off the manhunt now."

There was a clatter and a muffled, "Fuck." After a minute Turner came back, breathing a little harder. "Thanks, man. The little shit was halfway down the drainage ditch. Your eagle eyes saved at least that family's day."

There was a reason Jason didn't usually get his cell phone out during shift. It'd have to wait until he got relieved for lunch.

He was walking back from the cafeteria, brain half busy going over the definitions he'd read, the other half still scanning for anything unusual—impossible to turn that habit off—when his gaze caught on a group of people in front of outdoor stage C: a handful of actors and stunt people presumably going over that evening's shoot. But what the fucking hell was Arkady doing smack in the middle of that group?

As if he'd shouted the name out loud, Arkady turned and waved with a wide smile that hit Jason straight in the solar plexus and nixed his very ability to draw breath. He had to sternly tell his lizard brain to let more intelligent parts handle this. He caught sight of Natalya behind the men, then, pointing at something on the stage. So she was probably giving her brother a private tour.

He was still standing undecided, stupidly rooted to the spot, when Arkady came over to him.

"I'm getting the VIP treatment," he called out halfway. Then, when he reached Jason, he said more quietly, "And I'm getting into character."

He stood that perfect fraction too close that would shout to anyone watching that he was trying to hide intimacy; and he leaned in when he murmured, "So, this is where you work."

Jason had the hardest time not to touch him and pull him in even closer. He quickly jammed both hands in his pockets.

Arkady seemed to have gotten over his jet lag, and was bouncy and excited and way better at this acting game than was good for Jason's peace of mind. His murmur had been downright seductive. Knowing that it was an act didn't help one bit against the shivers it was sending across Jason's skin.

"Want to show me in more detail?" Arkady asked in that same tone, but with such an exaggerated wink this time that it broke the spell.

Jason laughed. "Watch it, buddy. You're lucky I work in a restricted area, or I'd show you *detail.*"

At that Arkady's eyes grew intent. Jason bit his tongue. Too much? Were there any rules in this game beyond not getting caught? How outrageous was too outrageous?

Arkady threw a glance over his shoulder as if to see whether they were being observed. "You wanted things public, right?" He licked his lips, and Jason could see him swallow hard. "And we only have four weeks. Which means we need to move things along." His eyes were a little wider than usual.

What the—

Then Arkady went down on one knee and held a wide steel band out on his palm. "Want to take it and put it on while they're still looking over?"

Whoa. "A heads-up would have been nice."

"Why? Stunned suits you."

Jason didn't grace that with a reply, took the ring, and slipped it on his finger. It was a tad large, but a good fit for Arkady having to eyeball it.

The crowd in the back erupted into cheers as Arkady got up and put his arms around Jason's neck. He didn't go for the kiss, as Jason had expected, but merely touched their foreheads together. A pretense that would look like the real deal from where the guys were standing. He was so close, though. Jason had to take a deep breath to calm his heartbeat. He stepped back when the others moved in, but he took the congratulations and slaps on the shoulder in a haze. As if he wasn't part of the whole thing, but merely watching it, like in a dream.

Everyone had entirely too much fun with the idea of a wedding and wanted to be a part of the planning. But Arkady easily fielded questions about the where and when of it, laughed at quips about the speed of their romance, and noted down event suggestions and tips for venues and stuff like that on his phone. He moved among these all-American boys as if he'd been born here; hell, he was even losing his accent already. Next to his easy cosmopolitan grace, Jason felt like a hick.

"I, uh . . ." Jason hooked a thumb over his shoulder at the office building and half turned to leave, but Arkady slipped an arm through his and pulled him off to one side a little.

"When are you getting out of here?" Arkady's murmur was back, and this time he didn't wink.

Jason tried to swallow, but his throat was dry. "I'm starting my second shift at two, so not before ten."

Arkady's face fell. "Guess I'll have to keep myself entertained until then. Don't dawdle, I'll be waiting for you. I have a proposition for you." Again that eyebrow wiggle. But this time it only made Jason more aware of the possibilities in that last sentence.

He cleared his throat. "Gotta get back to work," he croaked.

The fear of stumbling was too ingrained to allow him to run, but he'd had more dignified exits, that was for sure. He really had to remember that they were playing a role. Keeping that in mind should not have been this hard. It had been his own plan; Arkady was just following it. But *a proposition*? Said in that tone of voice? Jason firmly clamped down on all the different scenarios his mind came up with, because if he allowed even a fraction of that head-porn to play, his concentration would be toast, and he could kiss his job goodbye.

Still, by the time he made it home that night, he was equal parts wary and on tenterhooks about said proposition.

Arkady, however, was curled up on the couch in faded jeans and a laundered-to-death T-shirt, beer in hand, engrossed in a documentary about some sort of rodent, so Jason left him to it and went upstairs. All he wanted was a shower, and to get the prosthesis off; it had been a long-ass day. But it would be more of a bitch to put it back on after a shower than to keep it on. In the evenings he usually didn't bother, but he'd be damned if he was going to hobble around the house on his iWALK while Arkady was living here.

He sat on the bed, suddenly tired and out of options. He was used to being alone. This whole arrangement had been a lousy idea. He should call it off. Just go tell Arkady he'd changed his mind, and to take his money and find someone else. He made it halfway to the door before his head cinema started up, playing him the scene where he was trying to explain to his daughter why she hadn't gotten the education she deserved because her father hadn't been able to deal with having a roommate.

He paused and stared at the door from where the muted cadence of the TV-narrator turned into the drone of a eulogy. The next scene in his head was him talking to Natalya at her brother's funeral after some skinheads had kicked his skull in. *Wish I could have done more to save him, but the chafing from my prosthesis was just too unbearable.*

His skin crawled; he shook himself like an animal does to get vermin out of its fur. That head cinema was a double-edged sword. When he'd been a boy, it had given him loving parents and doting grandparents. As a soldier he'd used it to relieve boredom, and to anticipate every possible thing that could go wrong during a mission. But it also tended to pop up with worst-case scenarios or ugly truths when he didn't need or want them.

You're a fucking prize, Cooley.

That wasn't head cinema; that was his old drill sergeant's voice. *Now get your fucking head out of your fucking ass and do your motherfucking job.*

Right. He straightened his shoulders and went back downstairs, concentrating on each step. Tired and stairs didn't go well together in his world.

"What proposition?" he asked as soon as he stepped into the main room.

Arkady barely took his eyes off the screen, just stretched his arms above his head and said with a yawn, "Oh yeah, like I said, I'm a handy guy to have around and would be happy to pitch in with the renos. I have a vague idea what you've been trying to do with the room, so I drew up a plan for you. Do you want to see it? To check how close I am?"

Jason listened to his heartbeat in his ears, waiting for the rest. An eternity went by before he realized that there was no *rest*.

"That's it?"

Now Arkady did look at him, one eyebrow up. "What did you think it was? An indecent proposal?"

For a second, Jason thought Arkady was enjoying this, his discomfort, needling him. "Fuck you."

"What? You did, didn't you? Listen, I know you said the reno wasn't worth it, but it sure beats the hell out of staring at the wall. And you also said it bugs you. I'm trying to help." He seemed half-exasperated, half-puzzled now. And, really, why would he play Jason for a fool? He didn't strike Jason as the sadistic type.

Not that Jason knew all that much about the man, but his instincts were usually good. Plus Arkady had everything to lose here if he pissed Jason off. But the reno came with too much stuff he couldn't even explain when he was wide-awake. Much less when he was tired and had no clue which of the thoughts zinging around in his brain was important and which wasn't.

"Yeah, okay. Look, I'm tired, just . . . Thanks, but no, thanks." He fled back upstairs and into the shower for real this time. Only after he'd turned the lights out did it occur to him that he'd forgotten to eat dinner. Fuck his obsession with propositions, fuck his head cinema, and fuck Arkady in particular.

Okay, there was a thought he hadn't needed spelled out.

CHAPTER SIX

"**Y**ou okay?" Natalya asked from across the breakfast table.

"Sure." Arkady's reply came automatically, brain busy with the puzzle that was Jason Cooley.

"Because you've been watching your cereal get soggy and your coffee get cold." She tapped his forehead. "What's going on in there?"

"*Nichevo.* Nothing. Zero. It's five in the morning. Brains are dead at five in the morning. Everyone I stay with here is way too obsessed with getting up at dawn. Normal people sleep at this time. I don't even know how Anna made it out the door half an hour ago; she scares me. Jesus."

Natalya didn't say anything, but didn't take her eyes off him either. Damn her. He didn't even last two minutes, before he couldn't fight the grin anymore. She'd always managed to make him feel a little sheepish. "You know me too well. How do you still do that after all these years?"

"You haven't changed. Now, answer the question."

"Jason has this old house, his grandparents', and he started to fix it up the way he likes it but doesn't have the time. So, last night I offered to help, and he about took my head off." He frowned into his cereal. "And I have no clue what I did."

"Maybe he's embarrassed about not getting it done himself? Men can be touchy that way," she added with a wink.

"Funny. No, I don't think that's it. He was perfectly open and unembarrassed about it before. Only said it wasn't worth it when I offered help. I thought he meant my time. But I have more than enough of that, so I drew up some suggestions. I mean, he's busy, and I'm not. Right? He didn't even want to see them. Just, boom."

Maybe it hadn't been about the renos at all. Maybe it had been about what Jason had assumed he was going to say. Whatever that was. But that made no sense either, because then he'd have blown up *before* he realized Arkady *wasn't* coming on to him. No, it had to be about some invisible boundary Arkady had overstepped. "He's such a weird mix of lonely and not letting anyone in. He guards his privacy like a dragon with a treasure. Part of that is the leg thing, I think, but there's something else too, something—I don't know—deeper, maybe."

"You've thought a lot about him. Are you falling in love, Kashka? Forgetting this is just make-believe?"

His heart did a double beat. "No way. Not a chance."

When she didn't say anything, he added, "So not interested."

Still nothing. Then the steady tap-tap of a nail on the tabletop.

He threw her a quick look. "Come on, I'm not falling for a straight guy."

"He's straight, then?"

"Yeah. I asked."

Head cocked to one side, she nodded slowly. "Uh-huh."

"What?"

"You're so not interested that you asked him if he was gay?"

Nonono, it hadn't been like that at all. Had it? *Fuck.* He wolfed down his soggy cereal until he couldn't stand the silence anymore. Damn her and her interrogation tactics. "Did you know he has a kid?"

One of her eyebrows went up. "Nope. Do tell."

"Apparently that's what he needs the money for. She's a cutie, about Irina's age."

"You've met her?"

He made a face. Yeah, that was weird, that she hadn't been over, because Jason clearly cared about her a lot. But maybe she came only once a month or something. "No. He has her picture on the fridge."

"So he's divorced?"

Arkady shook his head. "Never married."

"Or so he says." The chair creaked when she leaned back hard. "You better make sure."

"Wait, I thought you trusted him?"

With narrow eyes she said, "Yeah, before he was about to break my little brother's heart."

"Lay off!" The spoon made a loud *clang* as he threw it in the bowl. "That is not going to happen."

Her lips formed a hard-pressed line, keeping in any further argument as she got up. She was definitely not happy, but there was nothing he could do about that now. She would just have to wait and see. Because it wasn't going to happen.

They spent the morning in Port Angeles, where Tasha had some friends. She took him to Vic's Café and introduced him to the people she knew there who spoke Russian and who, she said, might help him with his homesick blues. He didn't contradict her, even though his blues had more to do with leaving family behind than with leaving Russia. Or, at least, Putin's Russia. Seeing fresh faces might do him good. And he'd always enjoyed coffee shop crowds.

According to Tasha, they were a changeable community, loosely connected through language and culture, but very much the rebels and the disenchanted. Political dissenters, draft refugees, queers, punks, freethinkers—people who, had they not left home, would eventually have found themselves in jail. Some of them had been jailed in the past; some had gotten out by the skin of their teeth; some, like Arkady, had left before things got dire.

Most of them lived in and around Port Angeles, though not all in the same neighborhood; others occasionally visited from Seattle and even from across the Canadian border. There was a Russian language center attached to the Peninsula Academy, a private college those with enough money sent their children to, but the real hub, where everyone met at one point or another was Vic's.

Vic—tall, bald, with one gold earring—could have been cast in a Mister Clean commercial. He was Latvian, not Russian, and he made it clear every opportunity he got that the café was neutral ground. If you entered here, you left your national, religious, and cultural differences and enmities at the door or you'd find yourself booted back into the street very quickly. Vic ran the place with laid-back efficiency and a bone-dry sense of humor. Arkady instantly liked him.

When Tasha and he walked in, Vic was discussing the terms of catering a fundraising affair with a woman who negotiated like tempered steel. Tasha introduced her as Yelena Mikhailovna.

"She runs Vanin Enterprises. They do import/export. And I have no idea what else," Tasha murmured when they sat down with their coffees and sandwiches. "I think she eats people for breakfast."

That from Tasha, who was far from a pushover herself.

Vic and Yelena seemed to have reached a compromise, despite the tough negotiations, because they soon came over for amiable gossip about people Arkady didn't know.

"Has your daughter arrived yet?" Tasha asked at some point.

Vic rolled his eyes. "Next week. Don't remind me."

Yelena snorted. "Afraid of a teenager?"

"A teenager whom my ex-wife describes as needing 'her father's firm hand.' Also," Vic stared tragically into his coffee. "My love life will be fantastic. Like a unicorn. They don't exist either." He got up to serve a couple that had sat down at the far end of the room.

The next time the door opened, Tasha waved to the man who came in. "Grigory, come, meet my brother Arkady."

Grigory was short and trim, with a beard like an English lawn, and flamingly gay. He kissed Tasha and Arkady on both cheeks, and gave Yelena the kind of stare people reserved for spiders and scorpions.

Yelena laughed. "I have to get going anyway. Duty calls. Don't worry, *dushka*, I won't get married a second time, you have nothing to fear."

"Grigory's a wedding planner," Tasha explained. Her intense eye contact said, *I'm giving you a hint here.*

Arkady took a second to get it. "A wedd— Oh. Right." He turned to Grigory. "We need to talk."

Arkady walked away with the feeling that he'd made some friends he could come back to. The thought partly filled a hole he hadn't been paying attention to, because it had been expected. Because he didn't do well without ties, and still missed everyone back home like crazy.

So, finding friends was like a new beginning. A real one, that would hopefully survive a fake marriage.

Tasha helped him rent a small car that wouldn't break the bank and left him fiddling with the GPS on his new phone, because she had to get to work. He had to stop spending money, or get a job. Jason still hadn't asked how much he'd be paid for his *services*, but Arkady felt like he was using up money that no longer belonged to him. Not once he had the slip of paper that would allow him to stay, anyway.

With that thought came the fidgets. He was trying his damnedest to operate under the assumption that he would get the green card, but it was by no means a given. Everything could go wrong at any moment. And then he'd find his ass back in Russia. A gay man in a jail cell. God help him. *Stop that. Concentrate on the road. Think positive.* Easier said than done, though. Things were moving, but not fast enough. At the back of his mind lurked the uneasy knowledge that he wouldn't be able to keep up the charade forever. Or even long enough.

That night he prowled about Jason's kitchen and living room, trying to shake the feeling that he needed to speed things up, that he needed to do something. Right now.

Jason stood leaning against the counter, patiently waiting for the *ding* that would let them know their lasagna was ready.

When Arkady passed between him and the table, he laid a hand against Arkady's chest and pointed at a chair. "Sit. You're driving me bonkers."

He was as still and relaxed as Arkady was wired, his hand radiating warmth that Arkady wanted to lean into. Instead he took a step away from temptation and turned to take the indicated seat. "Sorry. Cabin fever, I think. I'm not used to having nothing to do all day. I should try to find a job."

"You can't." The *ding* came, and Jason maneuvered the plastic tray from microwave to counter and carefully peeled the top off. "Not legally. Not until you've filed your papers and had them approved."

Arkady stuck his tongue out at Jason's back. "I wasn't planning to scream it from the rooftops." He idly watched the play of muscles under the T-shirt as Jason divided the lasagna up between two plates.

"If you get caught—" Jason set the plates on the table and took the other chair "—you can kiss your green card goodbye."

There were so many rules, known and unknown ones. They made the whole process seem like a minefield. One wrong step, one crossing of an invisible line, and he'd be blown to pieces. How could a person know all the rules? Did anyone? How many applicants failed? Were they meant to fail? To hold off his rising panic, Arkady latched on to the flash of anger that last thought brought with it.

"Well, I need to do *something*."

"Are you already done playing tourist?"

Arkady shrugged. You had to be in a certain mood to play tourist, and he wasn't. He wanted to do something meaningful, something targeted, not gape at the ocean and buy trinkets with money that was earmarked for the biggest event in his life.

"What do you want to see or do?" Jason asked between bites.

"What are my options? What do you typically do in your free time?"

"Eat? Sleep?"

Arkady rolled his eyes. "Come on. Beyond that. I know you work a lot, but even you have to get away sometimes."

Now it was Jason's turn to shrug. He did seem to have a hard time coming up with something. "I have a pint now and then," he finally said. "Or drive up to Seattle to see Lily."

"How often do you get to see her? Doesn't she stay with you every so often?"

Jason's eyes widened. He seemed horrified by the very idea. "I go when I can get away. It's a long drive." He didn't even answer the second question.

"I'd love to meet her."

Jason froze for a moment, then said slowly, "I don't think that would be appropriate."

Arkady's hackles rose. The *Too gay for your daughter?* was on the tip of his tongue; old defenses were hard to demolish. But then he swallowed the challenge. Because this was Jason, who'd given him no reason to be defensive, who was hard to get a rise out of in any case. And he was right in that it wasn't appropriate. Arkady had forgotten—it was too easy to forget—that they were only pretending a relationship. He nodded. "Point taken."

Again Jason shrugged, and this time it seemed to be an apology. Maybe to take the sting out of his rejection, he said, "Sometimes I drive up to the ridge. For a bit of target practice. It's—"

He caught himself up so hard that Arkady was instantly dying to know what he'd been about to say. *It's what? Quiet? Illegal? Not much?* Jason wasn't looking at him, and Arkady suddenly knew without a doubt that he'd just hit on a chance to get to know the big man better.

"I haven't fired a gun in years. Be interesting to know whether I can still hit a target. We could pack a lunch, make a day of it if you can get away from work."

"I can get away." Now Jason was watching him, and Arkady wondered what he was seeing, or what he had caught in his voice. Hiding anything from Jason Cooley was extremely hard; he was an uncanny observer . . . He'd be hell to buy Christmas presents for. The thought made him snort, and Jason tilted his head in an unspoken question. Arkady waved it away. "Never mind. Not a bit relevant. Do we have a date, then?"

"I guess so. Day after tomorrow?" Jason added after a pause, maybe checking a mental calendar.

Arkady nodded. "Day after tomorrow, it is."

They left early. Jason seemed incapable of sleeping in, which, Arkady groused silently, was definitely a deeply black mark against him. At least he served Arkady coffee and a warm breakfast. Apparently Jason's cooking skills extended to bacon and eggs, which was more than Arkady could claim for himself.

Once they were on their way, he leaned back and slept in the car, since Jason always drove in complete silence anyway, and this early in the morning even Arkady couldn't be bothered to try to get a conversation going. But when he did open his eyes again, he was struck by the beauty of the landscape they were driving through, and by how much it reminded him of home.

"Looks almost like the woods around my parents' dacha," he murmured. Only at Jason's uncomprehending stare did he realize he'd spoken in Russian. "Sorry." He sat up and gestured out the window. "The trees and everything reminds me of where I grew up."

"St. Petersburg?"

"No. Petersburg is the big city, it's work and culture and nightlife; it's nice and all. But this? This is like home." *I could get used to this.*

Jason parked the car at a trailhead and handed Arkady the backpack that held coffee and sandwiches. He himself grabbed the two gun sacks he'd stored in the trunk before they left, then led the way up the trail. It was easy walking at first, but after about half an hour, Jason left the trail and they had to pick their steps through the trees and some underbrush. Jason used every handhold he could find and stepped very deliberately, especially with his left leg. Arkady watched him closely, but to his own detriment found that the terrain didn't slow the big guy down much. As the hillside steepened, Arkady was soon sweating and out of breath. But just when he was about to cry craven and ask for a break, the invisible path Jason was following leveled out again and soon after opened into a clearing almost the size of a soccer field. A log sat on the ground at the far end, but Arkady didn't see any bottles or cans like people typically used for target practice. He set the backpack down and watched Jason unpack one of the rifles, the make of which Arkady didn't recognize. It looked old, but well-maintained.

"I take it you know how to use one of these?" Jason asked.

"One of these as in 'in general'? Yes. That particular one? No, but I'm pretty sure I can figure it out."

"Show me." Jason handed him the rifle, then watched him take it, weigh it in his hand, open the straight-pull bolt to check whether it was loaded—it wasn't—and peer into the barrel.

"Cleaned both of them last night," Jason said, "but you're welcome to redo it."

Satisfied the gun wouldn't explode in his hand, Arkady shook his head and sighted along the barrel at the log. When he turned to Jason again, Jason held out a box of small-caliber rounds and watched as Arkady fed one into the chamber.

"What are we shooting at?" Arkady asked.

"Depends. How good of a shot are you?"

"Like I said, it's been a while, so I'm guessing. At this distance? Something the size of an apple maybe?"

Jason nodded, then set off along the edge of the clearing, scanning the ground. He bent over and picked up a few pieces of wood, which he sat on top of the log. Arkady waited until he'd made it back to his side, then checked down the barrel once more. Damn, the targets looked awfully small from here. "Anything I need to know about the gun?"

Jason took it from him, aimed, and fired. The leftmost piece of wood disintegrated in a spray of splinters.

"Nope," he said, and handed the gun back. Great. No pressure.

"Anything back there?"

Jason grunted, whether annoyed or satisfied, Arkady couldn't tell. "Just a few yards of trees, a drop, and ocean."

Arkady reloaded and tried to remember every rule his dad and uncle and later the army had pounded into his head. He pressed the stock against his shoulder, wriggling a little until it felt comfortable, exhaled, aimed, and fired before his arm could get tired. The second piece of wood did a summersault off the log along with a few splinters of the log itself.

"Too low," Arkady commented on his own shot.

"Not bad. Not bad at all. You'll do."

For some weird reason that praise warmed him from the inside out, even though he didn't have the foggiest idea what he'd *do* for.

"Finish the row. Get your feel for it back," Jason suggested.

Three pieces remained on the log. On his second shot, Arkady overcompensated and missed the target completely, but pulverized it with the next shot. The last two disappeared on the first try each.

Jason nodded. "Let's make it a bit more interesting." He pulled the backpack toward himself and dug a paper bag out of one of the side pockets. He opened it and let Arkady take a peek. Chestnuts. Interesting indeed. Jason set ten of them on the log. Five on each side. Looked like they were taking turns, then.

"Standing?" he asked when Jason came back.

"You can kneel if you want to. I don't mind. I don't kneel well."

Standing, then. "You first." That would give him an idea of what he was up against.

Jason unpacked the other rifle—also old, worn, a different make than the one he'd given Arkady—checked it over, and loaded it with a stripper clip. Then he stood at a slight angle, brought the gun up against his shoulder, and fired, almost without aiming, five times in a steady sequence. One chestnut remained on his side of the log.

So at least it was interesting for him too, and not just a game to keep Arkady happy. Good. He might actually have a chance at this. He reloaded with the stripper clip Jason gave him, shifted his own stance a little, and brought the gun up to his shoulder. *Exhale, aim, fire. Don't worry about the shot going wide, just keep aiming and firing down the line.* He managed to hit two of his chestnuts, and turned back toward Jason with a shrug and a grin he found mirrored on Jason's face.

"Haven't shot in years, huh? You're going to make me feel bad."

Echoes of memories floated up from the depth of his mind. Of long summer days in the woods. Of playing this game against Misha and Tasha.

He'd been afraid this might bring back his time in the army and all the baggage associated with that, but it hadn't. It had brought back way better things. He felt good. Jason was clearly the better shot, but Arkady still didn't suck.

"Best of three?" Jason suggested, and Arkady nodded. He expected to lose all of them, but now he was sure he could give Jason a run for his money. "What are we shooting for?" he asked, and thought, *A kiss.*

He turned and looked at the log to hide the flush he could feel blooming in his cheeks.

Jason grunted. "Winner gets first shower."

"You're so on," Arkady said, laughing.

He did end up losing all three rounds, by an only slightly better margin than the first one. Jason packed up the rifles, then grabbed the backpack and waved it at the log. "Makes a good seat for lunch," he said.

Arkady followed him, marveling at the fact that even on this difficult terrain, he'd never be able to tell that Jason wasn't walking on his own two legs.

"You're good with that, you know?"

Jason half turned. "I had a lot of practice," he said, and Arkady realized he was still talking about shooting.

"Your leg, I mean."

Jason flinched. His voice dropped half a register when he repeated, "I've had a lot of practice."

Arkady knew it was a difficult topic, but if they continued to dance around it, it was sure to trip them up sooner rather than later. "Still."

"Better men have returned to active service after losing a leg." Jason had stopped in front of the log without turning. His tone was even, but his neck muscles stood out like bridge trusses.

Arkady took a deep breath and plowed ahead, hoping his torn-apart body wouldn't be found in the woods later by a chance hiker. "Better how?"

Jason's hand curled hard around the strap of the backpack. "Let's eat," he said, in that same even tone. Then he turned, slowly lowered himself onto the log, and stretched his left leg out in front of him.

Arkady hesitated, watched him dig the thermos and sandwiches out. All Jason's signals were telling him to back the fuck off, but he might not get a chance again.

"You're dealing with an appalling injury better than I've ever seen. And I've seen a few."

Jason silently held out a sandwich until Arkady took it, then pointed at the log. "Sit. Eat."

They ate in silence, passing the thermos cup back and forth. Slowly the birdsong started back up around them; the noon sun hit the clearing from directly above, sending up a fragrant wave from the needle- and leaf-strewn ground. Even in the dappled shade at the edge, the heat was enough to make Arkady comfortably drowsy. He played a little game with himself: every time Jason passed him the cup, he'd turn it to drink from the spot where Jason's lips had touched it. Close enough to a kiss to send tiny delicious shivers down his spine. He felt like leaning against the big body by his side, just to relax in the flickering sunlight, but he doubted he'd be able to sell that as *practicing his role*. Plus he wasn't done prying. "Better how?"

"Huh?" Jason sounded as drowsy as Arkady felt.

"You said, 'Better men have returned to active service after losing a leg.' How were they supposedly better?"

Jason took a deep breath, and Arkady held his, though he suddenly realized, he wasn't really expecting Jason to get in his face or slug him, because that simply wasn't the type of man he was. "Well?"

"Arkady—"

"I know, I know. You don't want to talk about it, but think! Isn't that exactly the sort of thing I should know about you if I'm asked?"

Jason crumpled up the sandwich wrappers and stashed them, then he tapped the upside-down cup against the trunk they were sitting on. *Tap-tap, tap-tap,* pause, *tap-tap, tap.*

"Point," Jason finally conceded. He screwed the cup back on the thermos and shoved it into the backpack. "Better able to deal with how it messes up your head, I guess."

"The loss?" Arkady asked carefully. He wasn't sure what Jason meant, and wanted to keep him talking.

"Phantom pain." Jason stared at his outstretched leg. "It's much easier now. The mirror helps. And physio, of course. But at the time when I still had the chance to get back into active service, it was crippling enough that everyone was convinced I'd never work again. So I took my discharge." He barked a laugh. "You wouldn't believe how badly something can hurt that isn't even there anymore."

"I've heard about it. How does the mirror help?"

Jason shrugged. "Mirror therapy. You hide the crap leg behind a mirror that shows you the good one. It kinda tricks the brain into seeing the missing limb as still there. I have no clue why that stops the pain, but sometimes it does."

"Pretty cool. I had no idea. Weird things, brains, huh?" When Jason didn't say anything, Arkady went on. "Why did you want to go back into active service?" It was the one thing that didn't make sense to him. He could barely understand why anyone would want to be a soldier in the first place, though he supposed that Jason's family history had something to do with that.

Jason threw him a look that said he was asking the obvious. "It's what I do," he said. "It's my job."

"You loved it, then?"

Jason paused for a moment. "I don't know about love. It was a good job. I was good at it. Only thing I was ever good at. Only thing I know, in fact. I signed up out of high school." He shrugged. "There isn't anything else."

It was said matter-of-factly, definitely not fishing for compliments. But it was so manifestly untrue that Arkady couldn't help himself. "What about your job now?"

Another one of those joyless barks. "Staring at TV screens all day long? That's not a job; it's a pain in the ass. Literally."

Arkady laughed. "I can believe the last one. But from what your colleagues say, you're good at that too. Reading people? Drawing the right conclusions? I'd already noticed how good you are at quickly analyzing situations. It's a valuable ability."

"Yeah, right, earns me minimum wage every day."

"Why do you stick with that?"

"Are you fucking with me? Look at me. I'm lucky they hired me in the first place. Who hires a cripple?"

"Except you're not."

"Huh?"

"Crippled. You're not crippled." When Jason opened his mouth, Arkady pointed at his outstretched leg. "Yeah, I'm not blind, but think about it. So, maybe you can't jump out of a plane, maybe you won't win a race. Mind you, I'm not betting on either, but even if you can't, there aren't many men who can, and most of them have perfectly satisfying jobs."

Jason snorted.

"What?"

"Which part of 'I joined out of high school and didn't learn anything else' did you miss?"

"It's never too late."

"Dude. I'm the guy marrying for money, remember? I can't afford time off to go to school. And I couldn't pay for school if I did."

"Don't go to school, then. Work as a security adviser. I'm willing to bet you can walk into a building, scan the lobby for five minutes, and tell them all the ways in which their security sucks."

"So?" It came out mostly defensive, but there was a hint of curiosity too.

With a smug grin, Arkady said, "People pay good money for that."

"Maybe. From someone competent."

"Seriously? Man, you exude competence. I mean look at yourself. You're quiet, no-nonsense competence on legs."

"Plural?" Jason deadpanned.

"Sorry. But I mean it. You're exactly the kind of guy I'd—" Arkady's heart beat in his throat when he realized he'd been about to say *marry*. As in *for real*. The sudden adrenaline rush made him dizzy.

Jason was watching at him, head tilted to one side, a bemused expression on his face.

"Hire," Arkady spit out. "If I was a company. With a security issue. You're exactly the guy I'd hire."

Jason nodded slowly. Arkady was sure his lapse hadn't gone unnoticed. Not with Jason it hadn't. But he wasn't sure how badly he'd been busted.

"Appreciate the endorsement." Jason got up and stretched. "I'll think about it." His tone said that wasn't bloody likely.

Arkady gazed at that powerful figure limned in sunlight, and shook his head. "I don't get you. Everyone around you believes in you, even my sister—and Tasha's really hard to impress. Why can't you believe in you? What happened?" He couldn't see Jason's face against the light, but there was no mistaking the sudden stillness. One heartbeat, two.

"I guess we're done here." Jason picked up the backpack and his gun. "Or do you want to shoot some more?"

Clearly the, *We're done here,* was not about target practice. "I'm good," Arkady said. "For now." He wasn't talking about target practice either.

They walked in silence back to the car the way they had come, with Jason in the lead. Yup, quiet competence summed it up rather nicely. The kind of man you wanted to have your back. Or share your life.

Better take it easy, Kashka. Listen to your big sister, and don't get your heart broken.

CHAPTER SEVEN

Jason didn't see Arkady for the rest of the week, not awake, anyway. Arkady had found a cheap rental car and was usually still out when Jason came home, and still asleep, like now, when Jason left for work.

But the day in the woods stuck in Jason's bones. He didn't blame Arkady for asking about his leg. Arkady was right: it was exactly the sort of thing that would come up. But the questions had been hard to answer. They always were. The leg was his to deal with, and dealing with it was more complicated than he could find words to explain. Weirdly though, he'd found that he wanted to explain all of that to Arkady.

Both hands wrapped around his coffee mug and both elbows on the breakfast bar, he stood contemplating the tousled head above one flung-out arm, long fingers relaxed in sleep. Under the blankets, Arkady had one knee drawn up, but the other foot stuck out over the end of the couch. Guilt unfurled in Jason's chest when he thought about the king-sized bed upstairs. But he wasn't ready to go there. Sleeping next to a man wasn't even the issue, though he wasn't sure how much sleep he'd be getting next to this particular man. But dropping his pants in front of anyone, man or woman? Or worse, handling the prosthesis? Skin care? No, he was definitely not ready to go there.

At least Arkady hadn't pitied him. But calling him competent? *Competent, my ass.* Jason didn't know the first thing about approaching anyone to do any sort of business with. He'd barely managed to get his application together for the job he had now. *Security advisor* might sound enticing, but it was way out of his league. And damn Arkady for putting the idea in his head and making him think about it.

He finished his coffee and grabbed his gear, careful not to wake the sleeping prince on the couch.

That night, when he came home, Arkady's car was in the drive. It'd been a long-ass day, and he'd been looking forward to conking out on the couch with a beer and a movie, but for some weird reason, seeing the car made him feel less tired.

Male voices from the kitchen greeted him when he opened the door. That explained the blue Honda he'd passed at the curb.

Arkady looked up and smiled when Jason stepped into the kitchen, and that smile, too, did unreasonable things to his insides.

The other man was short and wiry with a well-groomed beard and a way of moving that immediately registered as *gay* in Jason's brain. He had to wrestle down a surprising need to snarl as he realized that Arkady apparently had a social life, and who knew what else.

Both men got up, and Arkady came and hugged him, giving him a significant eyebrow wiggle when he said, "Hi, honey. This is Grigory Petrovich Sidorov. He's a wedding planner."

Jason blinked.

"Greg will do," Grigory said when they shook hands.

But it hadn't been the name that had made Jason blink. "I'm sure I can remember Grigory."

"He's going to take care of all our wedding plans," Arkady said, then added with an exaggerated wink only Jason could see, "Isn't it romantic?"

"Quite." That might have come out a little drier than was good for them, because Arkady was obviously giving his visitor a performance. But to say Jason was surprised didn't do his feelings justice. He felt like he was trying to wrestle a car at full speed through an S curve, while it kept breaking out and skidding sideways.

"It is going to be quite a challenge, of course." Grigory's accent was noticeable, but not heavy. "Since the wedding is in two weeks and you haven't planned a single thing yet." His tone and raised eyebrow implied an inconceivable offense.

Jason shrugged. "We go to the office and sign papers. What's to plan?"

Grigory turned to Arkady with an air of disbelief. "You were not joking."

Arkady's answer was a helpless shrug.

"What?" Jason snapped. The feeling that they were ganging up on him was hard to tamp down. He needed to get a grip, though, because Arkady, at least, was clearly playing a role. A role Jason had suggested he play. *He's not mine.*

The thought was like a dagger in the dark, and Jason quickly slammed a lid on it and all its baggage. Of course Arkady wasn't his. That had nothing to do with anything. It had simply been a long day, and this whole wedding gig had taken him by surprise.

Grigory turned back to him and ticked an item off his thumb. "One. Suits. Arkady here might get away with wearing one off the rack, though he's tall. But you, my friend . . ." He walked around Jason, shaking his head with an air of regret. "I'm afraid there's no way."

Before Jason could even open his mouth to say he had a perfectly good suit in his closet that he'd only worn twice at funerals, Grigory ticked off the next item on his index. "Two. Venue. Unless either of you can pull some serious strings, you're going to have your wedding in a third-class burger joint."

Jason gathered that was an offense in line with simply signing papers wherever one went to sign these things.

"Three. Catering. With that I might be able to help, though I'll have you know that I'll be calling in some serious favors."

It began to dawn on Jason that they were not talking about an intimate service here.

"Four. Officiant. Everyone wants to get married in the summer, so, again, I'm going to have to give you a hand. Which reminds me, have you written your vows?"

Jason narrowly avoided a spit take.

"No, we'd like to go with the traditional wording as far as possible," Arkady cut in smoothly, and Jason could have kissed him, in a perfectly not wedding-related sort of way.

"A traditional wedding, got it." Grigory had immediately taken up the ball and was running amok with it. "Ribbons and flowers, a natural look, nothing too cutesy. Three-tiered wedding cake." He threw another one of his accusatory glances at Jason. "In two weeks."

Jason decided this was an excellent moment for a strategic retreat. "Why don't I let you two put your heads together without me cramping your style."

He pulled Arkady close and placed a chaste kiss on his temple. "You know what I want, love."

Whether Arkady was too surprised to protest or happy to comply, he let Jason get away with grabbing his keys and heading out the door. A solitary pint would definitely be better than whatever those two were cooking up in his living room. *Natural ribbons, my ass.*

For some unfathomable reason, though, that solitary pint turned out to feel very lonely indeed. Which was weird. Jason was used to drinking alone. Had been ever since he'd come back here. He liked it that way, and he saw no reason why that should have changed. Certainly no blond, blue-eyed reason. Especially one who dragged wedding planners into the house. Gay wedding planners, damn it. Unfortunately, he had to admit that Arkady was playing his part to perfection. A traditional wedding with all the trimmings would help their plan way more than the bare-bones affair he'd had in mind. But only if Arkady didn't start running around with other guys while trying to convince the world he was in love with Jason. It placed the mission outcome in jeopardy. That was the reason Jason was feeling snarly. Whatever. It didn't really matter why. He should go back and pretend to be useful. Keep an eye on things. With a sigh, he drained his glass and heaved himself to his feet. With a bit of luck Grigory would already be gone.

But by the time he made it back, the planning session had merely proceeded to full swing, it seemed. His kitchen table had been taken over by an army of notes and binders, from color samples to one that seemed to hold nothing but an array of business cards.

"What flavor?" Grigory asked him as soon as he stepped in the kitchen. Jason tried to keep his eyebrows from creeping up into his hairline. "What are my choices?" he asked, and immediately regretted it when Grigory fished a long list out of the pile and opened his mouth to read from it.

"He'll want lemon," Arkady said.

Jason, still mystified, promptly gave him two thumbs-up and a big smile.

"Lemon it is." Grigory ticked a line on his list and shoved the sheet of paper into a folder, then flipped a page on the notepad in front of him. "Music," he said. "What's your song?"

Jason turned to Arkady again for help, but this time all he got was a shrug.

"Opening dance," Grigory said with more than a hint of impatience in his voice. "You have to have a song. Something romantic, or cheesy, or both that has a special meaning for the two of you?"

All Jason had heard was, *Opening dance*. The rest was white noise. "No dance." He was not going to make a stumbling fool of himself at his own fake wedding.

Arkady had been tapping his teeth with a pen, but at that he got up. "Give us a minute, would you?" he said to Grigory, before turning Jason by the shoulders and maneuvering him into the living room.

"I mean it," Jason said. "I'm not dancing."

"Look." Arkady's eyes were gentle, which made Jason flinch, because he just knew it was to soften a blow.

"I see you walk nearly every day, take the stairs, drive, even run if you have to. So don't tell me this is about any physical inability to set one foot in front of the other." He paused, but Jason was still running through his reply options when Arkady went on, "So, it's about playing it safe."

Before Jason could protest the implication that he was scared, Arkady raised his hand. "I get it, I do. I'm all about playing it safe." There was a bitterness in that last line that Jason couldn't place. "But believe me, people will expect us to dance, and if we don't, they're going to ask why. If you're trying to shift the focus away from your prosthesis, I expect this will do exactly the opposite."

That was hard to argue with. Jason could easily see the friendly proddings followed by concerned questions. *Not feeling it* wouldn't cut it. Still . . . Again he looked to Arkady for help, and Arkady came through.

"We'll pick something slow. We'll make it one of those full-hug-shuffles people who can't dance resort to the world over. You won't stumble. And you sure as hell won't fall. I won't let you. I swear."

Jason had to swallow the sudden lump in his throat. "M'kay," he got out, torn between feeling sheepish for having been so easily read, and moved beyond words that Arkady had not only seen the problem and wasn't judging, but was giving him a way out as well.

"So," Arkady said with a soft smile. "What song?"

But Jason's brain was busy picturing Arkady's arms around him while they were softly swaying to music he couldn't hear.

"Don't worry, we'll find something." Arkady walked back to the kitchen, and Jason found himself staring at his ass. He tried to shake himself out of it. What the fuck was wrong with him? He didn't get drunk from one beer. He watched Grigory pack up his stuff, and stayed rooted to the floor as Arkady brought the wedding planner to the door, where they said their goodbyes. The house had been silent for a while when he looked up and saw Arkady leaning in the doorway with a bemused smile on his lips. They just stood there, looking at each other. Jason's hands grew warm, then his whole body.

Arkady finally went over to the stereo and knelt to pull out a CD. Strands of hair curled around his bent neck, almost long enough to touch his shoulders. Jason reached out to caress the bowed line of his head and neck, and only at the last minute curled his fingers into a fist, shoved it in his pocket, and took a step back.

When the first chords of Beyoncé's "Flaws and All" started playing, Arkady stood up and closed the distance, then came one step closer. He took both of Jason's hands and placed them on his shoulders.

"Just checking if this works as I think it will," Arkady murmured. He slipped his hands around Jason's waist and started shifting his weight side to side in rhythm with the music, then stepping from one foot to the other.

Jason had a sudden flashback to prom night, to dancing like this with Kendra, and what it had led to later that night. But it wasn't a clear image; the memory had become washed-out over the years. And now it faded even more, overlaid with Arkady, here and now, the way his muscles moved under Jason's hands, the way his eyes caught the light, the blond stubble on his jaw.

Jason fought down the strong impulse to kiss him again. It hadn't been welcome the first time, it wouldn't be now. They weren't dancing for fun. He had to remember that. This was mission prep, nothing else. And yet, his body had begun to move along with Arkady's. Inch by inch their feet followed an invisible circle on the floor, Jason on the inside, Arkady covering the slightly larger outer perimeter, his hand warm against Jason's back, there to hold him should his artificial leg catch on a crack in the boards.

God, he was so close, barely a handspan between them. It would be so easy to lean in and to—

The music ended, and with a deep breath, Arkady let him go. Or had that been a sigh? *Wishful thinking, Cooley.*

"See?" Arkady said. "That didn't go too badly, did it?"

Jason shook his head. Words were buried somewhere under a bunch of stuff he had no name for. He mentally kicked himself. He had no *use* for that stuff either. Because that was the other thing he had to remember: He had nothing to offer. Nothing anyone had ever wanted. Not his parents or grandparents, not Kendra, and certainly not Arkady. The only time he'd ever been of value to anyone was in the army. If he wanted to be of value to Arkady, he had to remember that Arkady was a job to do, a mission to complete. No distractions.

"It'll work, I guess," he said out loud, his voice grating against everything he didn't say. *Let's do another song. Let me kiss you again. Let me . . .* He shoved both hands in his pockets and stared at his feet, anywhere but those clear blue eyes that had just now had the slightest frown between them.

There was a long pause, then Arkady asked, "Am I pushing too hard?"

At that Jason did look up. And there was more than a slight frown now. There was insecurity in Arkady's eyes, and worse, hurt. *Fuck.* Like kicking a puppy. And Jason knew what that felt like. Not the kicking, but the being kicked part. Being pushed away, not wanted. Whatever he'd been thinking about went down and disappeared in the depth of those blue eyes.

"No." He cleared his throat. His voice still sounded like shit for no good reason. "No. You're right. Dancing will be expected."

He wanted to smooth that frown out. Instead he bent and pressed the back button on the CD player, then held his hand out to Arkady. "In fact, let's do it again. Just to make sure."

Arkady didn't hesitate for a second. He fitted himself easily against Jason's body, and with a wink and a smile, wrapped his arms around Jason's neck.

So much closer than before. Heartbeat against heartbeat. Blue eyes with beginning sun marks around the edges. Blond hair curling around an earlobe and under the chin. The impulse to brush it back irresistible.

At the touch, Arkady leaned his head on his arm, nose against Jason's neck. Funny how short of breath such a small gesture could make a grown man feel. And how hard it was to remember the rules of this game. That it was a game. Playacting. Pretend. So hard to remember. What if he allowed himself to believe? For just a minute, just one song, to believe that there was someone who wanted him close like this? He shut his eyes and leaned his head against Arkady's, let his body do the shuffle-sway on automatic, and pretended that he was wanted, pretended that there was somewhere he belonged.

Just for one song.

He didn't know how long they moved like that, but when Arkady gently straightened and stepped back, the room was quiet. Had been quiet for a while, Jason realized. The song had long ended. All he wanted was to restart it and get back to where he'd been a minute ago.

"Flaws and All," huh? Had Arkady simply pulled a random CD out, or had he picked the song on purpose?

Suddenly the day and the beer he'd had conspired to pile the weight of the world on Jason's shoulders. He should eat a bit and go to bed. Or just go to bed.

But when he turned to drag himself upstairs, there was Arkady, watching him with half-raised eyebrows. "Are you okay?"

"Fine." Going to bed this early would put the lie to that, wouldn't it? "Wanna show me the wedding stuff while I nuke some dinner?"

A lopsided grin appeared on Arkady's face. "You say the most romantic things."

Jason shrugged. The quip deserved a retort, but his brain was blank.

He shoved a couple of TV dinners in the microwave and, over food he didn't taste, okayed everything Arkady put before him. What did he know about decorations and cakes, catering, venues, or seating arrangements? It seemed like a lot of money for nothing, but Arkady assured him they'd kept it on the lean side, and apparently Arkady had already made some friends who'd likely help out for free. Jason had nothing and no one to add to that, either.

The last sheet of paper in front of him was titled *Guest list.* It had *Grooms' Attendants* at the top, and Arkady had put Natalya's name down.

Underneath was a list of names—some were *Wolf's Landing* crew, most Jason didn't recognize. Arkady had been here three weeks. How did he know ten times more people to invite to a wedding than Jason did after growing up here?

"Who's going to be your best man?" Arkady asked.

Good question. The only one Jason could think of was Mark. "I'll ask a guy I know." Not a friend.

It had always been easier to keep people at arm's length, because they would leave anyway, but right now it felt like he'd been missing out.

He wrote down Mark's name with a question mark, and then Jack Daley in the guest list column, because Mark wouldn't want to come alone, would he?

For good measure, Jason added Jack's sister, Margaret, as well, then he was done.

It was a pitifully short list.

"Your father?" Arkady suggested.

"Not a chance in hell. Even if I wanted him there, which I don't, he wouldn't come to a gay wedding." Jason tapped two names on Arkady's list. "Your parents going to fly in?"

"I'm not sure. The tickets aren't cheap. Tasha and I might try to rig something with Skype and iPads. We'll see. I do want to ask them, but I don't want them to pay for tickets they can ill afford for . . ." Arkady sighed and vaguely indicated the jumble on the table.

"A fake wedding," Jason finished for him.

"Yeah. Which reminds me, I asked Grigory to put a note on the invitations that we don't want any wedding presents. That, if people do feel compelled to spend money, they should make a donation to their favorite charity instead."

Jason frowned, but Arkady gave him a helpless shrug. "Nothing at all would seem funny."

"Fair enough." Only it wasn't. None of this was. When he'd made the decision to help Arkady get his green card, he hadn't anticipated collateral damage. *Lousy planning, Cooley.*

Arkady picked the guest list back up and stared at it hard. "Your daughter should be there," he said, without looking up.

Jason swallowed the immediate no that rose to his lips. He didn't get to see her that often, and by the time she was old enough to understand marriage and divorce, the wedding and Arkady would be a distant memory. He took a deep breath to get rid of the sudden tightness in his chest. "She might enjoy throwing petals or flowers from a basket," he said, and wrote down Lily's name. And then Kendra and Dan, because they wouldn't just leave her in his care, would they? It didn't feel right, regardless. But maybe they'd have something else going on, or they just wouldn't care to come.

Six names. Still not a lot. "I can ask some of the guys at work." There was no one he particularly wanted there, but it couldn't hurt to put the word out. People might feel slighted otherwise, since he'd be asking Mark, and Arkady would be inviting crew as well. Jason had no idea what the protocol was for a wedding. Not for a real one, and sure as hell not for a fake one.

CHAPTER EIGHT

Grigory had done an amazing job with the wedding decorations. He'd stuck to the traditional, as they'd asked, but had managed a classy, almost masculine style, like something straight out of the *Gentleman's Journal.* The white gardenias in lapels, on tables, and on the ceremony arbor only served to emphasize that style.

Arkady couldn't keep his eyes off Jason. Not that it was easy at any time, but today, in a three-piece tailored suit, all that intense, quiet power barely contained under an expensive veneer of polished sophistication, he looked downright devastating. It took Mark stepping between them to congratulate Jason and razz him about something, before Arkady was able to turn away.

People were taking their seats in the rows of chairs, Tasha was busy with setting up an iPad on a wheeled contraption that would allow their parents to be part of the ceremony. Everything was well taken care of, and for a minute Arkady managed to tune out the buzz around him and concentrate on breathing.

Until a tiny guest in a pale-blue dress and tiara with a braid down her back came toward him. Arkady had nieces just a tad older than her, so he recognized *Frozen,* or *Cold Heart* as it was called in Russia, when he saw it. She curtsied, then held out her hand. "I'm Lily Reines, Jason Cooley's daughter. It is so nice to meet you."

Jesus, God, had Jason said his kid was five? She was taking his breath away all over again, a thing that seemed to run in the family. He went down on one knee to shake her hand and be at eye level. "*Enchanté,* Miss Reines. How wonderful to finally see you in person. Jason has a picture of you on his fridge, but I have to say, it doesn't do you justice."

Lily giggled, then pointed to where two adults were taking their seats. "I'll be over there, with Mom and Dad."

"See you at the dance, then. I hope you'll save one for me."

She turned briefly on her way over to her parents to wave, then scrambled onto a chair.

They'd decided against the whole scattering of flowers or petals thing in an effort to keep it simple. He almost regretted that decision now. She would have been perfect. He was in love.

So why, then, was his heart so heavy?

Because she wasn't part of Jason's life, because Jason, the tough guy who pushed all his buttons, wasn't a family man. He'd had a family and walked away from it. And even if Lily had been in Jason's life, she'd never be in Arkady's. Because this, none of this was real. He really had to remember that. Just not today. If he wanted to survive today, present a happy face to the world, he had to try to lose himself in the moment, in the stunning tough guy waiting for him at the end of the aisle. Today, he had to lie.

"You may now kiss the groom."

It was supposed to have been just a quick kiss, a peck to satisfy conventions. For the photo op, and to give the people who'd come to the wedding something to talk about should they ever be interviewed by immigration.

But when Jason's hands framed his face, Arkady made the mistake of closing his eyes. This time he'd expected the big man's remarkable gentleness; he'd been ready for it, but that didn't work in favor of his control. The soft touch of lips on lips sparked its way into his system that much faster. This was no dark-alley doorway, no jeering crowd; the wedding venue and the people they had invited provided as safe a space as one could hope for. He could let himself melt into the kiss without fear, and he gave up any attempt of trying to resist it. Not with a man who knew how to kiss so well, but who didn't take anything Arkady offered for granted.

The hoots and applause from the crowd, the camera flashes that were reduced to red flickers through his eyelids, all fell away along with any vertical integrity his spine might have possessed at some point. But Jason's arm caught him and held him tight. It didn't feel like a stage kiss at all, but like a promise. The thought jolted him back onto his own two feet, right when Jason gently disentangled himself.

When Arkady opened his eyes, he expected to see his own confusion mirrored in Jason. But instead Jason's eyes were shining with a soft smile, and, just for a heartbeat, Jason laid his hand against Arkady's cheek before he turned to the cheering crowd and bowed, laughing. Arkady quickly followed suit, hoping to God he was hiding how shaken he was better than he thought.

He managed one more glance at Jason, so dangerously handsome in his tailor-made suit, before they were stormed by congratulations, hugs, and handshakes, and the obligatory kisses from the Russians in the crowd.

Food was served, toasts were offered, the cake had to be cut with Jason's and his hands touching on the knife, more flashes from the photographers, and Jason's smile unchanged. It was everything a real wedding should have been. Then Jack, who'd agreed to DJ for them, put on Beyoncé's "Flaws and All," and there were calls of "Dance, dance!" from the crowd.

For a second Jason froze in his chair, and Arkady could see the play of his jaw muscles as he gritted his teeth. But then he got up, and, as he had done in his living room, offered Arkady his hand.

It had been easy to dance when they'd been practicing. Alone. Here, surrounded by family, his and Jason's, by new friends, and by acquaintances that could turn into friends, it suddenly became a symbol of their lie. Because they *were* lying. To all of them. Were repaying all that love and acceptance he'd so badly wanted in his life with deceit.

He took Jason's hand more to steady himself than anything else, and let himself be pulled onto the dance floor. Not that he could have done otherwise. They'd said their vows. *Lies, lies!* What was done was done.

When he looked at Jason, the radiant smile was gone, replaced by a frown of uncertainty.

"It's okay. I'm okay," Arkady said automatically. Why the hell was Jason frowning at his hesitation? It wasn't like they were real lovers. Husbands. Whatever. So, why was there that confused pain in his eyes?

Or was Jason merely afraid that Arkady might get cold feet, kick everyone out, and hurt them even more? Hurt his own chances at a green card into the bargain?

Get real, Izmaylov. He can't read your mind.

Nevertheless, Arkady found himself avoiding those searching eyes, because Jason was such a keen observer that his scrutiny was as good as mind reading.

Jason pulled him close, and Arkady didn't protest. Hiding his face against Jason's shoulder was a good way to avoid everyone's adoring expressions. Behind his closed eyelids, though, the barrage hammered away. *Lies. Lies.* Insistent. Rhythmic. But beat by beat, the words faded and merged into the thump of Jason's heart against his chest.

Jason's arms around his body. Holding him, shielding him. That didn't feel like a lie. It felt real. If he wanted it to be real, was it still a lie?

Fuck. Neither of them had any intention of keeping their vows. So yeah, still a lie.

Jason shifted his shoulders, making Arkady raise his head and look at him. Yup, that was definitely worry lining Jason's forehead and narrowing his eyes.

"I'm—" Arkady didn't get the *fine* out to finish his sentence, because Jason closed his lips with his own. Still gentle. But sure now. Surer with every kiss they exchanged. Stoking the embers of desire and need back to the conflagration that burned Arkady's more rational thoughts so fast that they might as well not have existed. The sound rising up in his throat was most certainly a moan, and there was nothing he could do to stop it. Fuck, he wanted this man with everything he had. When Jason came up for air, Arkady leaned in, chasing those lips and tongue.

But when he opened his eyes, he caught his sister's expression over Jason's shoulder—worried. Scared even. Shit, Tasha was never scared. He almost checked over his own shoulder to see what monster she might have seen behind him.

Jason ran a finger along Arkady's cheekbone, instantly distracting him. "I wish we didn't—

"Since our parents can't be here, may I claim the first dance, brother?"

It was called whiplash, and Arkady had it. His throat was so dry that he could only nod. He almost stumbled when Jason let him go. And here they'd been worried about Jason keeping his legs under him.

Half of his brain was screaming at him to pull himself together, the other half wanted to shake the rest of the sentence out of Jason. *I wish we didn't*— What? Couldn't Tasha have taken two seconds longer to cross the dance floor? *Fuck's sake.*

"Excuse me?" She sounded surprised more than irritated.

"Nothing." Had that come out loud? He tried to laugh it off, and led Tasha into the rhythm of the next song, when he could barely hear it.

"Staging an intervention, Sis?" *Keep it light.* It was the least he could do to make amends for his lies. Though the lie he was giving her was different than the one they'd been giving to everyone else. Now he did laugh. It was all so desperately funny. "Don't worry. Everything is under control."

"Don't you try that with me, Arkady Nikolayevich. You should see your face when you look at him."

Fuck. That obvious, was it? "It's for the cameras. I'm merely a great actor."

"No. That's just it. You suck at acting." Her face grew softer. "I know it's hard, doubly hard on a day like this, but if you don't keep that invisible line, you're going to get your heart broken." She briefly lowered her gaze to their clasped hands. "And it would be my fault. Don't do this to me, Arkasha, okay?" She was pleading with him now, and that was all kinds of wrong for his sister. "I couldn't— I don't want— Just don't fall in love with the guy, okay?"

This time he swallowed the laugh, because it felt too close to tears. But, held back, it collided with the *Too late!* his heart was screaming into the world, and some sound made it out, tearing up his throat in the process. He quickly turned it into a cough and a raspy "Okay" to Tasha, who was now busy whacking his back.

He was losing it, and he hadn't drunk that much yet.

That, however, was an omission easily rectified. He just had to bring everyone who came to congratulate, to tell him how happy they looked together, how cuuute they were, to the bar for a toast. Even his tolerance for alcohol had to mellow out under that barrage at some point. The vodka didn't dull the edge of his guilt as much as he'd hoped, but it did keep him away from both Jason and Tasha for most of the evening, and out of sight of the parental iPad setup, under a perfectly acceptable pretext.

Until the stream of well-wishers and drinking buddies dried up in the wee hours.

Until Jason materialized out of nowhere by his side, draped an arm around his shoulder, and said, "C'mon, sweetheart, time for bed."

Fuck. He had to say *bed*, didn't he? Like that didn't make Arkady imagine all the things he was trying so hard to ban from his mind.

He shrugged Jason's arm off his shoulder. "I don't need a nanny."

Vic behind the bar did a double take. *Shit. Keep up appearances. Make nice. But not too nice. Not too close.*

"Yeah, fine, I had a few," he conceded to amend his slipup. "There were a lot of toasts, you know. Don't get married every day." He watched one of Jason's eyebrows go up in something damn near to indulgent amusement, and sighed. "Lead the way. You're driving."

Jason called them a cab, though, so maybe he wasn't as sober as he looked. They sat in silence next to each other on the back seat, Arkady staring stubbornly ahead, conscious of Jason's occasional side glances. The vodka helped keep him in a thin bubble, but it made the lights swim in and out of focus. By the time they arrived at Jason's house, he was slightly queasy, irritated with the world in general and his decision to try this green card thing in particular, and he really had to piss.

He dashed past Jason in the tiny hallway, up the stairs, and into the bathroom, banging his shoulder against the doorframe because he was just that little bit too drunk for speed.

When he came back out, he ran straight into Jason's chest. *Déjà vu.* Only this time Jason was fully clothed, in the most devastating tuxedo, no less. And rather than letting go as quickly as possible, he held Arkady in a loose embrace. Easy to step out of. If one so desired. Arkady didn't move. He wanted to be kissed again, but he also wanted to punch Jason in the teeth for making him want in the first place. For not simply letting him go back downstairs and crash on the fucking couch.

As if he'd read his mind, Jason did let go, but only to frame Arkady's face with both his hands. The gesture that irresistible mix of gentle and sure that was so very Jason.

Arkady met his lips halfway, leaning into the kiss, hungry for it, for the heat of Jason's hands as they moved around his shoulder on one side and up into his hair on the other. For how their bodies fit against each other without stooping or reaching. For Jason's heartbeat against his chest. For the fire racing through his veins.

Dizzy with the kiss and the booze, he got tangled up in Jason's suit jacket, until it was shrugged to the floor.

They were stepping around each other, like they had dancing in the living room. A doorframe pressed against Arkady's back; a hand cupped his ass and pulled him close.

If there was a saint for gay men falling in love with straight guys, Arkady had never needed their help more than right now. Desire was pulsing through his body, pushing out what reason was left with every beat of his heart. "Straight men shouldn't be able to kiss like that," he murmured against Jason's lips when they broke for air.

"I might not be as straight as I thought I was."

It came out so softly that it was barely audible, but it washed through Arkady's veins like ice water. *What? The fuck?* Jason was drunk. Had to be. That line might even have come out a little slurred. Arkady couldn't afford to believe a word of it. *Keep your distance.* The warning glowed through the alcohol haze in his brain like a lighthouse beacon through fog, and he clung to it.

They were standing in Jason's bedroom, just past the doorway. Had that been by design, then?

"Is that so? Ready for a little wedding night fun?" The sarcasm cut through his fog. Hell, why not? They could have that at least, couldn't they? The passing thought that this wasn't how to keep the line, that there was all kinds of things wrong with his reasoning, disappeared as quickly as it had popped up, and Arkady dove back into the kiss.

Jason hadn't even tried to answer, was right there with him, kissing back, holding Arkady's ass with both hands, pressing their hips together, one hard dick against the other.

And why would he be hard if he'd only said he wasn't straight because he was drunk? There were no witnesses, no one else in the house to keep up pretenses for. So why kiss Arkady in the first place, unless because he'd wanted to? The *keep your distance* voice in Arkady's brain grew fainter with every one of those questions. He slid a hand between them to unbutton Jason's shirt, and stripped it off his shoulders. God, the man was just as ripped as he remembered from that brief instance on the landing. As he'd been in the fleeting hazy dream-bits that tended to stick around for the few moments of waking up.

They were both panting now, but unwilling to break the kiss, or Jason seemed to be. Arkady's body was more than ready to take things a step further. He fumbled with Jason's belt.

Jason broke the kiss and took a deep breath. "Um."

"Little help here?" He should have stopped a few vodkas earlier. If he'd known this was waiting at the end of the evening, he would have.

"I'm—" Jason stayed Arkady's hand with his own. Again with the whiplash. No, yes, no. What? With that, Arkady's earlier anger was back, and closer to the surface than expected. He tried to get his other hand between their bodies. Christ he was messed up; he needed to stop.

Jason shook his head. "No. Wait. I—" He caught Arkady's other hand as well and took a step back. He might have taken another step if he hadn't backed himself up against the foot of the bed.

Arkady tore his hands free. "Don't fuck with me." Anger, disappointment, and something way too close to pain were wrestling in his chest, throttling down his desire. An ugly laugh escaped past his lips. "'Not straight,' my ass. What then? Just a little gay? How much? That much?" He held his thumb and forefinger an inch apart in front of Jason's face. "Just enough to jerk me around when we're both drunk?"

Again Jason shook his head. "I'm not drunk." He hadn't raised his voice, but his hands were balled into fists against the sides of his legs, making the muscles in his arms and chest stand out to perfection. *Dear God.* "And I'm not gay. Just—"

"Just too straight to admit it."

"Fuck you."

"I wish," he hissed, cursing himself for not being in better control of himself, willing himself to sober up, wishing he'd not gotten drunk in the first place. Classic case of *It seemed like a good idea at the time*.

"Look," Jason said. "I— This was a mistake."

No shit. Arkady should get in his car and go— *Home, Izmaylov? And where exactly would that be?* He barked a laugh. Jason looked stricken. *Yeah, you should feel guilty for being an ass.*

Damn, Arkady should at least go downstairs and curl up on the couch. Sleep it off.

Instead he heard himself say, "Define 'this.'"

Jason shrugged, then moved his hand between them, indicating their mutual state of undress. Arkady suddenly realized that he, too, was missing his jacket, and that his shirt tails were hanging out.

"Coming on to you like this," Jason said softly. "When I obviously haven't got my shit sorted. I—" He stopped short, visibly fishing around for words. Finally he rapped his knuckles against his thigh.

For the second time that night, a cold wash of dread flooded Arkady's veins. "Fuck. Jesus Fuck." Puzzle pieces fell into place. No more whiplash. In fact, the whole back and forth made perfect sense. In a way. "This is about your leg?"

Jason hung his head without answering. But he didn't have to, because it was as clear as day which one of them was the real asshole.

"I'm an idiot, and I'm sorry." Arkady closed the distance between them and slipped a hand around Jason's neck. With their foreheads touching, he whispered. "I'm so sorry, Yasha. I'm sorry."

Jason simply stood there, but let himself be pulled in.

"Truth is, I'm the one who's drunk. And for all the wrong reasons." He laid his other hand against Jason's cheek, searching in his eyes for— He didn't even know what. Forgiveness? A solution? "Christ, this is messed up. I'm lost. *Prosti menya, moy drug*, I have no idea where we go from here."

Jason peered at him from under his brows. "After I made such a fuss about it, I guess there's no way you can just ignore the leg?"

"No." Arkady sat on the bed and patted the spot beside him. "Want to show me how it works?"

For long minutes, Jason stood looking at Arkady's hand on the bed. Only the muscles in his cheeks were jumping.

It wasn't easy waiting him out, to not move, not say anything else. But it seemed like a pivotal moment, and if Jason needed the time to *sort his shit*, he'd have it. Arkady had smashed enough emotional china today to last him a lifetime.

So he watched Jason's fists open and close, marveled at the play of muscles under the skin, noticed for the first time the small tattoo over his heart—a pulse line that spelled the word Lily in the middle, before resuming the pulse spikes.

He almost jumped when Jason suddenly slapped his thigh as if to boot himself into gear, then opened his belt and fly buttons, and stripped his pants down, giving Arkady the perfect view of his even more perfect ass. *Be still, my beating heart.*

Jason sat on the bed and methodically took his shoes and socks off, before struggling all the way out of his suit pants. It seemed fiddly to get them off over the prosthesis, and Arkady got the impression that he didn't usually do it this way. That this was for Arkady's benefit: laying it all bare. Jason's left knee and part of the thigh were covered by a black plastic or rubber sleeve that continued down over something like a socket that held what was left of his lower leg, the leg itself replaced by a gleaming steel rod with an artificial foot at the end. It struck Arkady as stark and utilitarian.

"Does it have to be black?"

"What?"

Arkady pointed at the sleeve without touching it. "It should be something more you. Camo. Or Ironman, or . . ." He opened his hands and shrugged. "I don't know. Whatever you're into."

Jason stared at him with raised eyebrows. "Really. I bare my fucking blown-to-pieces Achilles' heel to you, and the one thing you have to say about it is that it shouldn't be black?"

You're screwing it up, Izmaylov. Again. Think. Fast. "Well, unless black is what you're into. I guess. I mean, I wasn't judging. Or didn't mean to." He took a breath and shut up. It wasn't often that words failed him, but tonight he was missing the whole frontal cortex game. The more he tried to salvage whatever was left to save, the more of it he broke. Classic drunk joke. *Stop digging.*

But instead of getting mad or looking hurt, Jason laughed. And not just a short little laugh either, but a deep belly laugh, that grew into a bellow of mirth and . . . relief?

"What's so funny?"

"You? Me? I was afraid you might laugh. Or flinch. Or try extra hard to be matter-of-fact. Or even be, you know, too interested. Some people—" He shook his head, a flush creeping up his neck. Then he huffed a laugh. "I'd never in a thousand years have imagined you'd be offended the color of the sealing sleeve." That briefly set him off again. Then he said, "No, it doesn't have to be black. There are some funky ones, especially for kids. And some people wear custom jobs."

He paused, but Arkady didn't ask the obvious question, because he was sure that Jason wasn't finished. And he was right.

"I guess to me it's like a car. It has a job to do, and for that it doesn't need a fancy paint job or chrome rims." In almost a whisper he added, "Plus, no one ever sees it if I can help it."

It was like a blow to the solar plexus that admission, and what it meant that Jason had literally let his pants down today.

"You see it. Every day," Arkady said.

This time Jason's laughter was just a huff. "A neutral color makes it easier to ignore."

That, too, an admission. And still the very air in the room was heavy with unspoken things. By now Arkady was stone-cold sober. The emotional fireworks had burned the alcohol out of his system.

"How do you take it off?" He kept his voice matter-of-fact, technical. They both needed a break from the high-tension roller coaster.

Jason immediately caught on and answered in the same tone, as if explaining a new TV or power tool to him. "You roll the sleeve down over the edge of the socket to break the air seal." He did so while he talked, revealing a second layer underneath, a little paler than his skin. "Pull leg out of socket." He had to wiggle back and forth a bit to get his leg out of what resembled the upper part of a ski boot without the buckles. A silky material covered the second plasticky layer around the stump.

"You roll the sock off." He removed the silky material and hesitated again.

"Let me guess," Arkady quipped, trying to make it easier. "You then roll down that last piece. It's like the Dance of the Seven Veils."

Jason guffawed. "The Red Cross version. But yeah, you're right, roll down the gel liner, then wash or wet-wipe the stump, and put some lotion on it." He didn't get up immediately though, as if to give Arkady a chance to stare. Or was he daring him? To look or look away, though?

Jason's knee was crisscrossed with small scars that looked more jagged the further down the leg they went, to where the limb had been amputated slightly more than a hand's width below the knee. The skin around the stump looked red and a little irritated, probably due to the long day and several dances.

Arkady reached out to touch the knee, but at that Jason stood up on his one leg and reached for the door handle, leaning on it and a dresser on the other side of the door for a well-rehearsed swing-hop. "I'm gonna go take a shower." He stopped briefly in the doorway. "You don't have to leave," he said without looking back, then, with the help of the banister, crossed the landing to the bathroom. Arkady began to see how the tiny house worked to his advantage.

He listened for the sound of the water, then hefted the prosthesis Jason had left leaning against the bed. It was surprisingly light. He carefully set it back down exactly where it had been, afraid to break anything, afraid of leaving Jason in the lurch if he moved it somewhere else. The liner and what Jason had called a sock lay in a small heap on the far side of the neatly made bed with a nightstand on either side.

There was a second dresser under the window, a deep armchair in the corner, and the closet between it and the door. Both dressers and nightstands were fake wood straight out of the seventies, probably Jason's grandparents', the armchair maybe even older, and an undefinable color between red and brown. The boards under his feet were polished, and the wood had been sealed at one point, but scuffs revealed where people had been walking over the decades. No pictures anywhere, no books, no knickknacks. The curtains up here were as old and frilly as the ones in the living room.

He briefly contemplated opening drawers or doors for a peek, but what had seemed permissible with a stranger felt like crossing boundaries now, like betraying a trust.

When Jason came back, those thoughts went collectively out the window, because all the big guy was wearing was a towel. Water beads clung to the short hairs in the middle of his chest. He paused briefly in the doorway with a glance around the room, then took his sock and liner, pulled them straight inside-out and hung them from a rail attached to the end of the dresser. All that with minimal movements and perfect balance. He was stunning, leg or no leg, and he left Arkady's mouth dry.

Arkady waited for him to say something, to make a move, give him an indication, any indication of where they were heading, but he was probably just as clueless as Arkady was himself. The thought that they were caught in the most frustrating instance ever of the mannequin challenge made Arkady grin and broke his inner impasse. He stood and slowly opened the buttons on his shirt, then, just as slowly, took it off and placed it over the back of the armchair.

Jason watched his every move, but didn't call a stop. He might have been breathing a little faster, though.

When Arkady bent down to undo his shoelaces, he heard a strangled sound. He pulled his shoes and socks off and straightened, more light-headed than the brief stoop should have left him. Jason's gaze felt like a touch on his bare chest.

His slow movements had been intended to give Jason time to change his mind, but now they felt like he was doing a striptease. Heat rose up his neck at the thought, and to hide the blush, he looked down at his hands as he opened the button on his pants. But then he wanted to see Jason's face, needed to know his reaction to what he was doing.

Jason's eyes were fixed on Arkady's fingers pulling down the zipper, then on Arkady's hands pushing the pants down, on Arkady's middle when he stepped out of them and folded them over the armchair on top of his shirt.

The towel around Jason's hips was tented at least as much as Arkady's briefs now, and he sucked in his cheeks and raised his eyebrows in an unspoken question when his eyes met Arkady's.

"I have no idea." Arkady crossed the room and laid his palm on Jason's chest, framing the tattoo with thumb and index finger. "I'm making it up as I go." He searched Jason's eyes. "Tell me when you want me to stop."

"I don't want you to stop." Not even a hint of hesitation there.

"So then," Arkady skimmed his hand up Jason's chest, along his neck, cupped his cheek. "Tell me—" he kissed the corner of Jason's mouth, and watched his Adam's apple move as Jason swallowed "—how does it work, this not straight, but not gay thing?" He didn't really want to ask; there were answers he didn't want to hear. But he desperately needed to get this out of the way.

"Both," Jason breathed. "I mean, bi." He opened his eyes, a slight crease between his brows. "Sexual. I mean, bisexual. Me, that is."

Arkady laughed. "Yes, I gathered you were talking about yourself." His body was suddenly light as air. Everything was light. "And this is a recent development?"

"Not really, I don't think." The crease between his brows deepened; Arkady smoothed his thumb over it, and Jason relaxed. "Guess I've been a little slow connecting the dots."

"Mm-hmm."

"What?" Jason sounded half-doubtful, half-exasperated now. "I don't get to fuck until I slap a label on it?"

Arkady laughed. "No, man, but I'm swimming here. I'm trying to figure out direction, speed, and probability all at the same time. Give me a break."

"Sorry." Jason didn't look sorry, though. He looked like he was enjoying this odd dance they were dancing.

"So, you've played the field before?"

Jason cocked his head "Maybe. In a way. Not like you think, I think." He grimaced.

"Spell it out for me."

"Barracks," Jason said. "Too much testosterone, too little to do. Soapy handjobs in the shower. Getting head in a dark corner, that sort of thing."

"Only getting? Never giving?"

Jason shook his head, candid, as always, if maybe a bit embarrassed; a lesser man might have squirmed.

Arkady grinned and said with an over-the-top sigh, "Such high maintenance, masculinity, isn't it?"

"That wasn't— Wait." Jason squinted at him. "Are you fucking with me right now?"

Impossible to keep a straight face. Laughing, Arkady threw himself backward onto the bed, arms outstretched. "Punish me." He felt ridiculous, and more high than when he had been drunk earlier.

With a pivot, Jason dropped on the bed next to him. "I should," he growled, leaning on one elbow, his other hand hovering inches above Arkady's chest. "You're lucky I'm a bit . . ."

"Wet behind the ears?"

"Inexperienced." Jason rolled on top of him, bracing himself on his arms. "But I've always been a quick study." He moved his groin in slow circles, pressing down hard and sending hot pleasure zinging through Arkady's body until it came out in a low moan.

"Point made," Arkady panted. "Now shut up and kiss me."

Jason didn't need to be told twice.

Between the kiss and Jason's hips grinding against him, Arkady soon felt like his body was stretched across the universe, the tension in his balls deliciously unbearable. He pushed back, heightening the pressure as much as he could, until his balls tightened, and, just when he thought he couldn't take it anymore, the sweet, unbelievably sweet, relief hit. He groaned against Jason's lips, the tremors running through his body way beyond his control. And who'd want control, anyway, where surrender was divine?

He never wanted to come down from his high, but eventually his heartbeat calmed, and he opened his eyes to find Jason watching him. "What?"

"Nothing. Just getting to know you." A light kiss, then Jason rolled onto his back and wiped the towel he'd been wearing along his dick before tossing it through the door onto the landing.

"I'd better go shower too." It wasn't easy getting up when his limbs were heavy with sated desire, but it had been a long day, to say nothing of dancing, and stress, and booze; he sure needed that shower.

When he came back, Jason had moved under the covers. He lay on his back, hands crossed behind his neck, fast asleep. Arkady slipped in next to him and, after a moment hesitation, snuggled up against him, using his upper arm for a pillow. With dawn filtering through the curtains, he lightly ran his fingers over the short hairs on Jason's sternum until he fell asleep.

CHAPTER NINE

I t was past ten when Jason woke up, and for a second he thought his clock was off. He couldn't remember the last time he'd slept past dawn. But then the weight of Arkady's body on his left arm registered, and one by one the events of the day before flooded back.

He was married. To a guy. Who was now asleep on his chest. He'd kind of prepared himself for the first two as a transaction that had to happen to complete his mission: save Arkady from getting killed in Russia, and put some money toward Lily's schooling in the process. But that last one, that encompassed everything he hadn't been prepared for. Desire for one. Mutual desire at that.

He turned on his side so he could look at Arkady's face. The face of the man who had actually wanted him. It was hard to believe, but Arkady had had no reason to pretend. He'd had his wedding. And Jason had given him no reason to think he wasn't on board with the rest of the mission to get him his green card.

And no one had been watching them last night. Arkady could have gone downstairs and passed out on the couch. In fact, Jason had been sure that was what he was going to do. After clocking Jason for not keeping a lid on his shit.

Instead, Arkady had taken up the thread Jason had handed him and proceeded to unravel Jason, inch by inch. That was exactly how he felt: unraveled. He wasn't sure he liked it. There were parts of it he'd liked—hard to deny that. But it was also unsettling, and he didn't trust it. People just didn't stay in his life. If you did something right, people might like you, might acknowledge that you had something to offer, but in the end, they still left. And what he'd offered Arkady didn't require liking, or wanting to stay.

He carefully extricated himself so he wouldn't wake Arkady up. The poor guy would have the mother of all hangovers when he did. Better give him a few more hours.

Jason collected his stuff and went to take his shower, then dressed in the bathroom in sweats and a T-shirt. He'd been briefly tempted to use the iWALK, like he would have if he'd been alone. The skin around the stump could use a day's rest, but it wasn't too bad, and in the end he didn't feel quite at ease enough to do without the prothesis. Baby steps.

He made a pot of strong coffee and set up his laptop on the kitchen table, where he could connect it to the printer that was living a life of idleness in a recess under the breakfast bar.

He had a truckload of forms to print.

Arkady came downstairs two hours later, in the jeans he'd worn yesterday morning, before they'd gotten dressed up, and nothing else. He looked tousled and sleepy, and too good for words. The urge to take him right back upstairs and continue his exploration of Arkady's body was hard to wrestle down. But they had work to do.

"Do I smell coffee?" Arkady said. He didn't seem any the worse for having killed close to a bottle of vodka the evening before.

"Dregs. Let me make a fresh pot." It kept his hands busy, and his eyes off Arkady's ass in those jeans, and off the treasure trail that ran from his navel to behind the button.

"Thanks." Arkady started to walk over, but then stopped and bent over the table when he saw the pages. "Immigration? What're you up to?"

"Lots of forms to fill out. Better get a move on."

"Okaaay." He sounded wary, or maybe just tired.

"I have to be back at work tomorrow. Best make use of the free time. If we get them filled out today, I can post them and pay the fee tomorrow."

Arkady was riffling through the papers Jason had printed. "You're right. I didn't realize it was quite so much paperwork."

He came over to where Jason was measuring coffee powder into the filter, snuck an arm around his waist and kissed him on the side of the neck. "You should have woken me up."

Instantly electrified, Jason turned in his arm, coffee forgotten. "I thought you could use the extra sleep," he got out. There were other things he wanted to say and ask, but they crowded around in his brain until he couldn't make out a single one. At least Arkady had answered the question whether last night had been a drunk one-off. Apparently not. The possibilities left him breathless.

Arkady slipped his other arm around Jason, closing the circle. "Are you okay?"

"Affirmative." If Arkady was sober and still wanted him, he was more than okay.

"Good." Arkady pulled him close and kissed him. Softly at first, then, when Jason threaded his fingers through Arkady's hair, more urgently. Jason let himself fall into the kiss, because he could now. Boundaries had been redrawn last night. Kissing was definitely okay. It shot like lightning through his veins, and pulled at his ass muscles and his balls. But if he didn't stop now, there would be no paperwork today.

"Forms," he managed, breaking the kiss.

"Right." Arkady took a step back and combed all ten fingers through his hair. "What a shame, though." There was laughter in his breathlessness. "I could just eat you up."

"I better make us some eggs, before the worst happens." Jason kept his voice deadpan, but it wasn't easy in the face of Arkady's suggestively wiggling eyebrows.

He finished setting up the coffeepot, then got eggs, bacon, and bread out of the fridge, while Arkady had a proper go at the forms. "All those abbreviations are giving me a headache," he muttered.

Jason was still trying to keep his mind out of the gutter and not burn anything, including his fingers.

When he set two plates on the table, Arkady said, "We better mail everyone and ask for copies of the photos they took yesterday."

"Already did." Jason pulled the laptop toward himself to check his mail, and to keep his hands off Arkady.

"Aren't you efficient?" Arkady quipped, but Jason didn't have any breath left to answer him. Two people had already gotten back to him with pictures. One in an email, and the other had uploaded a whole bunch of them on Facebook.

Jason was staring at the image of Arkady and himself right after exchanging their vows. He had his hands around Arkady's face and was about to kiss him.

They looked like lovers. It wasn't just the fact that they were wearing matching suits and rings, or that they were standing under the gardenia arch. It was the way he was looking at Arkady. There was an energy to the photo that Jason hadn't expected could be captured. It was an intimate, revealing picture that stripped him bare of all pretenses and laid him open for everyone to see how he felt. It was what they'd been trying to pretend for weeks, but how a photo could capture something like that when it hadn't actually been there, Jason didn't know. Because it hadn't been there, had it? He remembered allowing himself to be happy, to be in the moment, to believe that they weren't taking advantage of everyone present. But that photo? That screamed *I love you*. "Huh."

"What are you grunting at?" Arkady said, but he was busy wiping egg off his plate with his toast.

For a heartbeat Jason was tempted to delete the picture. It made him feel naked in the same way that taking off his prosthetic leg had last night. Maybe it was all in his head, though?

He slowly turned the laptop so Arkady could see the screen.

Arkady fell against the chairback as if he'd been shot. "I'll be damned," he said softly.

"Good one, right?" Jason said, testing the waters, trying to figure out if Arkady saw what he was seeing.

"I'll say." Arkady looked as if he'd been caught with his hand in the cookie jar, which made no sense. "Tasha is going to have a field day with that one," he murmured.

"Huh?" Jason was officially lost.

For a heartbeat—two—Arkady kept staring at the image on the screen, then he shook himself like a wet dog. He beamed at Jason. "A field day, a happy day. Isn't that what you say in English? It's an excellent picture. Definitely one we want to print and include with our papers." With that, he reached across for the mouse and scrolled through the album. A pulse started beating at his throat, and he took a shaky breath. "In fact, we should include all of these. They're all good."

Then he cleaned the table and started to fill in forms, while Jason turned the screen back, reclaimed the mouse, and went through the rest of the pictures. They were all like that. The two of them kissing, dancing, cutting the cake—every image a declaration of love. He stared at Arkady's bent head next to him, trying to figure out what had happened to himself. Why he, Jason, looked like that in every picture. Yes, Arkady was attractive. Very. And, yes his kisses set Jason's blood on fire. But that didn't mean he was in love with Arkady.

Christ, they'd known each other for four weeks. That was hardly enough time to fall in love. Though, of course, that was exactly what they were trying to sell to immigration.

Arkady placed his finger to the line he'd started writing in. "Does a patronym count as a middle name?" he asked, and looked up, straight into Jason's eyes.

Jason tried to say something. What had been the question? His throat was too dry to swallow—he tried, but it didn't work. The answer, the real one lay in those clear, blue eyes. Yes, four weeks were enough time to fall in love. Because he had. God help him. He was in love with the man who'd married him for a green card.

"Jason?"

"Huh?"

"What planet are you on, my friend? You look like you saw a ghost."

"No, just thinking of something else. Patronym. Yeah, no. I don't think so."

Arkady nodded, but he was still staring at Jason like he'd expected a different answer. "Okay. That's what I thought," he said slowly, then went back to writing. But after a few moments, he slammed the pen on the table. "Listen, I've said it before, and I meant it. I'm not trying to make your life difficult by living in your pocket."

He raised a hand, cutting off any reply Jason might have made. "I know, I know. We need to do this right. And we will. But while there's no reason why we can't have some fun in the process, I have no intention of going back on our deal to leave you in peace as soon as I have that card. You have to believe that. In fact . . ." He got up and disappeared in the hallway for a few seconds, before coming back with a tan envelope that he held out to Jason. "This is yours now."

Mystified, Jason took it and ripped it open. It was full of cash. Several thousand dollars at first glance.

"Thirteen thousand," Arkady said. "There was a little over fifteen, but I had to dip into it for the wedding. Sorry about that."

Jason nodded. He should say something, but his throat was so tight that nothing came out. Deal. They'd made a deal. And he'd just gotten paid. Everything as it should be. He could send the money to Kendra now. She could make a down payment for Lily's tuition. This was good. This was excellent.

"Thank you," he finally managed.

"No," Arkady said. "Thank *you*. With all my heart." He waved a hand toward the laptop. "Ignore those photos. They'll do what they're supposed to. That's it." Then, looking back at Jason, he said softly, "Okay?"

Again, all Jason had was a nod. And no idea where the sudden pain came from, or what to do with it. No idea what Arkady had just said. Not really. But he knew instinctively what Arkady needed to hear. "Okay."

"No intention of going back on our deal" and *"have some fun in the process"* played on repeat in his head.

"Great," Arkady grinned at him. "And promising."

Jason tried an answering grin. He didn't quite get why Arkady thought he suspected him of *going back on our deal* or what the photos had to do with that. Unless Arkady was telling him not to get his hopes up? But why then would *he* assure *Jason* that they could have fun with no strings attached? No, he didn't get it. What he did get was that this was still about the green card, with some bonus fucking if they both wanted it. Love didn't have anything to do with any of that.

So he picked himself up, buried the fallen, and gritted his teeth on the pain. That was what he was good at. He'd had a lot of practice. He even managed an answering grin, and a wink. "Just wait until we're done with this crap," he said, and it almost sounded as light as it was supposed to.

A couple of hours later, Arkady stretched his arms above his head and audibly cracked his back. "I've written my name and personal data so many times, they've lost all meaning," he complained.

Jason rubbed his eyes. "I vote for pizza."

"Seconded."

They agreed to share a large with everything, and Jason ordered online.

When he went to answer the door bell, though, it wasn't the pizza man, but Kendra and Lily waiting outside.

Kendra looked worried and harassed. "I'm so sorry, Jay. I wouldn't be here if it wasn't an emergency." Before he could reply, she repeated, "I'm so very sorry," at a point over his shoulder, and he knew Arkady was standing behind him.

"There were nuts in the pancakes," Lily said, as if that explained all. She squeezed past him, and said, "I had the French toast."

Kendra smiled after her, but it didn't erase the frown off her forehead. "Breakfast. Dan's in the hospital. Anaphylactic shock. I need to get back there. Can I leave Lily with you for a few hours?" She glanced past Jason again and blushed. "God, I hope I didn't interrupt anything."

It made Jason acutely aware that he was in sweats and Arkady was bare-chested.

"No, I— We just ordered pizza."

"Pizzaaaa!" came a jubilant little voice from the back.

"In fact, I thought you were the delivery guy. I mean, when the bell rang I thought— Do you want to come in?"

She shook her head. "I should get back. Are you sure this is okay?"

He had no idea what to do with a five-year-old for a few hours. "Of course it is." Or what to feed her. "Is she okayed for pizza?"

For the first time since he'd opened the door, Kendra's face relaxed. She even winked at him. "Just try to stop her." Then she hugged him, brief and tight. "Thanks, Jay. I owe you. I'll call you as soon as I know more."

"Yeah, yeah. Go, but drive carefully."

She was already on her way back to the car, and only acknowledged his warning with a wave over her shoulder.

Jason waited until she was gone before going back inside. Funnily, he felt more relaxed now. After this, the day *had* to be done throwing things at him. Which meant he knew what he was facing, which meant he could start to deal with it. You could google *children's entertainment*, right? You could google anything.

Lily was inspecting the premises. She wrinkled her nose at the torn floor boards, but declared the roughed-in breakfast bar, "Cooool."

She didn't seem overly worried about her dad. She told them she'd been in the hospital with anaphylactic shock only last year because of nuts, and it hadn't been that bad. She didn't even pause at the five-syllable word.

The pizza came a few minutes later, which meant half an hour down, occupied with eating. A total win in Jason's book.

Lily was a whirlwind; she got into everything. In the time it took him to discard the pizza box, she'd raced to the top of the stairs three times and discovered that she could slide down the banister on her tummy.

She also never stopped asking questions. "Is Arkady going to live here now? Can I stay with you until the end of the summer? Why is there a hole in the floor? Can I see your pro-static leg? Do you have any cake left from yesterday?"

Jason looked at Arkady over Lily's head. It hadn't occurred to him that they might be required to clean up the venue.

Arkady answered Lily's last question with a shrug. "I'm afraid I didn't pay attention. We could go check, I guess." He turned to Jason. "Or should we stay reachable here?"

It would be something to do. "I'll text Kendra. She knows where it is, so I don't see any problem."

"Caaake!" Lily screamed with both fists raised in the air.

Jason sighed. "You're going to be sick from junk food before the day is over."

But Arkady only laughed. "Kids have copper-plated stomachs. Even if they hurl, they simply keep going. Let me just put a shirt and some shoes on."

They all piled into Jason's car, but when they got to the wedding venue, found it locked up tight.

Lily pouted for about five seconds, but then announced they could go for ice cream instead. "What's your favorite flavor?"

"Pistachio," Arkady said.

Jason voted for chocolate. He hadn't had ice cream in years, and it was the only one he could think of.

"Mine is orange creamsicle. Can I have a waffle? I like your car. I get to sit in the seat like a grown-up."

It brought Jason up short. "Shit. Are you allowed to sit in a car without a booster seat?"

"You're not supposed to say 'shit.' It's a bad word," Lily said.

"Sorry."

Arkady buckled her up in the back seat, then said to Jason. "We have to get her home somehow."

"Fff— But on a straight route. I'll drop you off and go get ice cream," Jason volunteered, callously sacrificing Arkady as babysitter.

"Okay. You drive. I'll sit in the back with her. Sorry about that. I didn't think of a kiddie seat."

"Me neither. I've never had her in the car."

Arkady did a classic double take at that, but didn't say anything.

For some weird reason it made Jason feel defensive. He knew he wasn't father of the year material, but then, Lily had a dad, and a good one. And Jason did what he could in his own way, didn't he?

He listened to the two of them in the back seat while he was driving. Arkady had challenged her in a game of who could spot the most red cars, and they were currently arguing about whether orange counted as red. Lily won both the argument (orange didn't count as red) and the challenge. She was three cars ahead by the time they got home, and was only a little bit disappointed that she wouldn't get to go to an ice cream parlor in Jason's car. Jason bribed her with sprinkles and was absolved. He silently apologized to Kendra about all the sugar. He didn't know a lot about kids, but he was perfectly aware what healthy food looked like. Pizza, ice cream, and sprinkles wasn't it.

He found orange creamsicle and sugar sprinkles in the store but drew a blank on pistachio. Which might not be a bad thing. Lily probably knew enough not to touch nuts, but he felt safer not having any nutty flavors in the house. He bagged a double chocolate instead and hoped Arkady didn't have a cocoa allergy. On a whim, he added lube and condoms to his haul, trying not to question his motives too closely.

He came back to the spectacle of both Arkady and Lily lying on their bellies on the front lawn with their heads in the stamp-sized flower bed by the door.

"What the . . ."

"Shhh," Lily made with one finger on her lips. But then she waved him over. "Don't scare him," she whispered.

At first Jason didn't see a thing, but following Arkady's helpful finger, he spotted a small tree frog in a gap between two border stones.

"I'll put the ice cream in the freezer," he whispered in Lily's ear, and got a nod. Her rapt attention stayed focused on the frog.

In the end, though, he didn't have to wait long for them to join him. They came inside some ten minutes later, Lily beelining it to the fridge.

"Nuh-uh," Arkady said. "Hands." He pulled a chair up to the sink so she could reach it, and, clearly recognizing the voice of authority, she obediently washed her hands.

Arkady tied a towel around her neck, like he had for the pizza; he kept her engaged, answered her questions, and asked about a tree fort she was apparently building with her dad.

Jason could only stare in wonder when Arkady later showed her how to do magic tricks with a coin, and then kept her occupied with building and flying paper airplanes.

Kendra came to get her shortly after seven. "Dan is doing okay," was the first thing she said, "but they want to observe him overnight, just in case."

"You're welcome to bring Lily over for breakfast, while you pick him up," Arkady offered.

"Can I, Mommy, pleeease? Hospitals are boooring."

Kendra laughed. "Well, someone liked it here." She tilted her head and gave Jason an I-told-you-so look, but said "I don't think we'll need to bother you. Dan said he'd wait at the entrance."

"Sure," Jason heard himself say. "No problem."

When they'd left, he turned to Arkady. "Are you sure you don't have kids?"

"Positive. But I have an armful of nieces and a nephew." Arkady grinned. "Baptism by fire." Stooping to pick up the paper planes he asked, "First time she's been here?" His voice sounded carefully off-hand, but it felt like an accusation.

"It's a long drive," he said. "Much easier for me to visit her at home." And didn't that sound like a lie, when he only saw her awake maybe once a year?

After seeing her with Arkady, he suddenly felt like he was missing out.

"You okay, big guy?"

"I'm cool." He watched Arkady straighten and, turning to ditch the paper planes, almost trip over the torn-up floor board.

"Lily sure didn't like that hole in the floor," Jason said.

"Can I ask you something?" Arkady sat on the couch and stretched his legs under the table.

"Shoot."

"What's the holdup on the renos? Why don't you want to finish the place?"

Jason had his glib reply about not enough time and it not being worth it on the tip of his tongue, when Arkady added, "The real reason."

Jason shrugged. He hadn't really thought about it much. Trying to spruce the place up had simply felt useless. He stared at the yellow curtains, half expecting his grandmother's ghost hand to close the little gap that had been left by paper airplane traffic. "I just don't think anything I do is going to improve the house," he finally said. "It ain't home, never has been." Now there was a bitter truth. "I don't belong here. I've always been an intruder here. First I bombed my mother's career and then her parents' retirement."

"Come again?"

He didn't want to explain, but now that he'd started, he found himself unable to stop. "My parents were career soldiers. My birth was an accident—a disaster. It set my mother's career back by years. So she dumped me here with her parents and threw herself into the frontlines for quick promotion. Got herself promoted right past the pearly gates." He barked a laugh at his own joke. His bitterness surprised him. He'd always managed not to think about those garbage years. "Neither her parents nor my father ever forgave me for her death. Haven't talked to the old man since her funeral."

"How old were you when she died?"

Jason looked up, surprised. He'd forgotten Arkady was there. "Four. It's okay," he added when Arkady made a strangled sound. "I barely remember either of them. No love lost."

Arkady came over to put an arm around Jason's shoulder. "Upstairs." His voice was soft, but his tone brooked no argument. And truth be told, Jason didn't want to argue.

He let Arkady lead him upstairs and into the bedroom, lifted his arms when Arkady pulled his T-shirt over his head, and sat on the bed so Arkady could take his sneakers off.

Arkady left him to deal with his pants and his leg on his own, but wordlessly held the covers up for him when he was naked, so Jason could slip under the blankets.

Only then did Arkady strip out of his own clothes and join him. He still didn't talk; he ran his hand across Jason's face, making him close his eyes, then kissed him. But he didn't linger on the lips. He let his hands roam across Jason's body, warming the skin, and slowly kissed his way down Jason's chest and stomach—until Jason was breathing faster; until Arkady's hands weren't just warm anymore, but leaving trails of fire; until Jason's dick strained against his abdomen, and he bucked his hips in a wordless plea for Arkady's touch.

Arkady placed a line of kisses along his groin, then licked up his shaft and sucked him into his mouth. Pleasure exploded through Jason's body. It was all he could do not to buck, to let Arkady keep the lead. His finger curled into the sheets when the pressure built, then, suddenly Arkady let him go. Jason's eyes flew open. He barely swallowed the no that rose in his throat. Only a vestige of the sound made it past his lips.

"Got any lube and condoms?" Arkady asked.

It took Jason a second to find his words. "Downstairs. Walgreens bag."

"Aaand I guess that also answers my next question, whether you'd be okay taking this past the Princeton rub," Arkady said with a cat-ate-the-canary grin.

Jason felt the answering grin on his face.

He was still grinning when Arkady came back a minute later with the shopping bag and upended it on the bed. He was kneeling on the cover in all his naked glory, and Jason couldn't stop staring. He'd seen some built guys in the army, but no heavy muscles compared to Arkady's lithe beauty. Greek statues looked like that. "You're gorgeous."

Giving Jason the once-over, Arkady ran his hand up the inside of Jason's thigh. "You're not so bad yourself, my friend."

And the way he said it, contemplative and just a tad short of breath, Jason almost believed it.

"I want to ride you. Are you okay with that? You being all 'inexperienced'?" Arkady asked, his tone half-serious, half-teasing.

"I'm okay." He wasn't sure what to expect, but his imagination drove a wave of heat up his chest, and Arkady's hands on his dick when he rolled on the condom didn't help to cool him down.

Neither did the view of Arkady lubing himself up. Kneeling with his legs apart, body and head arched back, dick ramrod straight, he exaggerated the in-and-out movement of his arm, giving Jason a show. But if his harsh breath was any indication, he was also quite enjoying finger-fucking himself.

It was pure porn, and Jason could have jerked off to it in five seconds flat, but if he touched himself now, it would be over, and he very much did not want to miss out on what was next.

Kneeling upright, Arkady gave him the most lascivious look before he bent and kissed him, long, deep, drawing up a moan from Jason's chest. Arkady straddled him without breaking the kiss, then slowly rubbed his dick against Jason's stomach. Which meant on every push back, he was pressing against the crown of Jason's dick. Which— *Oh, gawd.*

Jason couldn't help himself; he lifted his hips, trying to follow when Arkady moved his body forward, and when that didn't work, grabbed Arkady's thighs and tried to push him back down.

With a soft chuckle, Arkady stayed his hands. "Yeah, me too. But I have to make sure you're ready."

There was nothing Jason could have replied. Nor did he need to: his body was screaming it out for him.

Arkady straightened and reached both hands behind him; Jason couldn't see it, but felt one hand wrap around his dick, holding him steady as Arkady slowly lowered his ass and just as slowly impaled himself on Jason's dick.

Tight! So very tight. The pressure rose unbelievably with every inch Arkady lowered himself. Jason started breathing in long gulps of air, desperately trying to relax, to keep himself from coming, to revel in the keen pleasure that was flooding his body. Then Arkady rocked up again. And back down.

Jason knew he was making sounds, could feel them in his throat, but he couldn't hear anything. Eyes closed, head back, lips slightly parted, Arkady was moving in a dreamlike rhythm that suspended Jason's senses. Stars shot through his body and exploded in front of his eyes.

Arkady sat up, grabbed the lube, and squeezed some into his hand. He closed it around his dick and started fisting himself, lazily at first, then faster, speeding up the rhythm with which he was fucking himself on Jason's dick as well. His breath came in short gasps.

As did Jason's. Every muscle in his body tightened with need, until his balls pulled up, and all that agonizing tension erupted in a series of blissful releases. Arkady's ass cheeks clenched around him, his body arched backward with a tortured moan, and his come covered Jason's chest and neck, echoing his own orgasm.

With a groan, Arkady pushed off him and collapsed next to him on the bed. Jason had just enough energy left to pull Arkady close against his body, then all he could do was lie there and listen to both of their heartbeats calming. Arkady buried his face against Jason's shoulder. In a perfect world, Jason would be able to whisper *I love you* against his husband's damp hair.

CHAPTER TEN

Once Jason had left for work every morning, there was nothing for Arkady to do, except to sit and watch TV or old movies, or stroll around town with way too much time to think.

The wedding—his mind steadfastly refused to label it *their* wedding—but even more so the day after, had left him unmoored. Of course, being a stranger in a strange land and having no routines to fall back on didn't help, but it went further than that.

He'd known, when he agreed to a green card marriage, that it was a potentially dangerous decision. Overstaying his visa, being at the mercy of someone he'd never met . . .

But the real danger had come from a completely different direction, and he'd been blindsided and overrun by a handsome, gentle giant of a man, who kissed like nobody's business, had a savior streak a mile wide, and yet couldn't save himself.

There were glimpses—dances, soul-baring talks, Lily's impromptu visit—of the relationship that might hold the key to Arkady's big dream: a family of his own. And in his weaker moments, he wanted to hold on to those glimpses with everything he had.

Tasha called a couple of days later to ask if he was okay. She didn't mention the photos. Because she hadn't seen them, or because she'd decided that all hope for him was lost after she had?

But after a while, she said abruptly, "You know, if you do love him, you should just tell him."

Whiplash again. "Whut?"

"Come on, Arkasha, I saw the pictures. Obviously, any further warnings to not fall in love are way too late. If they ever worked. So talk to the man. From what I've seen, there's a good chance he feels the same way."

But Arkady remembered how shocked Jason had been when he saw the photos from the wedding, saw image after image of Arkady staring at him with lovelorn eyes. And how he'd gone right back to his usual quiet self when Arkady had reassured him that he wasn't trying to hang on. No, a relationship wasn't what Jason had signed up for.

"No, there isn't," he said. "And even if there are sparks, that's hardly enough for a real marriage."

"Is that what you want?"

Eventually. "You know I always fall for the wrong guys," he said lightly, trying to close that topic.

But Tasha was difficult to distract. "Wrong how?"

"Lone wolves. Tough muscle. Hard cases. It's hot, but it's not— Okay, I'm not discussing this with my sister. I mean, he's not even trying to have a relationship with his daughter."

"And you know for a fact that's because he wants to be left alone?"

He didn't. For a long while he'd thought Jason wanted the opposite. "I have no idea. Look, I don't get fake married every day. I'm making this up as I go. I'll think about it, okay?"

"I just don't want you to get hurt."

"I know. I'll call you. Take care."

Nights were good. Nights had Jason, who turned out to be both more adventurous and more open than Arkady had expected after their tentative start. Arkady still didn't understand how his awkward reaction to the color of Jason's prosthesis sleeve had broken the ice there, but happily accepted that it had.

No, nights were nothing to complain about.

Days, though. Days were a bitch.

About two weeks after Jason had filed their papers, they received a receipt and a biometrics appointment for the beginning of September, the latter being, as far as Arkady could determine, an identity check and record.

Nothing too exciting, but it was a sign that things were moving in the right direction. It still didn't allow him to work, though, and he was getting antsier by the day.

Fuck, he needed to get out of here, at least for a few hours. Take his mind off things.

He left the biometrics notice on the table, where Jason would find it when he came home, grabbed a jacket and his car keys, and headed out the door. The August day immediately wrapped itself around him like a warm, wet washcloth, and he was grateful for the AC in the car.

It was even worse in Port Angeles. The parking lot behind Vic's shimmered in the heat, and Arkady's shirt got damp just from the walk to the front door.

It wasn't quite eleven yet, so with the morning crowd gone, and the lunch crowd not yet started, Vic's was deserted.

"I've put on a pot of tea," Vic said by way of hello. "Want some on ice?" The Russian consonants soft and lazy in the heat.

"Sounds great." Arkady plopped himself on a chair, and when Vic came over with a carafe and two glasses asked, "You okay? You look a little put out. How's Maya doing?"

Vic rolled his eyes. His daughter made him do that a lot. "Struggling. She has this course picked?" He shook his head. "I didn't realize quite how little English she has. She's enrolled in a remedial class at her college, but it's geared toward native speakers. It's a challenge." He took a sip of his tea and stared out the window. "What she needs is some intensive training with a private teacher." With a laugh he turned back to Arkady. "But who can afford that, right?"

Excitement ran through Arkady like an electric current. "I'll teach her." It'd be a far cry from a university lit class, but it would be something.

Vic shook his head. "I appreciate it, man. I really do, but I couldn't pay you."

"Oh yeah, remind me again how much you charged me for tending bar all night at the wedding."

"That's different."

"Bullshit. Besides, I couldn't take your money anyway. I don't have a work permit yet. Honestly, Vic, you'd be doing me a favor. I'm bored to tears."

"No shit? You're not just saying that?"

"I swear to God. If one more day goes by without me finding something to do, I'm going to take up origami. Or snooker."

Vic's face brightened. "You are so on." He held out his hand, and Arkady shook it. Vic pulled him in a bit. "And once you're legal and looking for a real job, send word. I know someone who knows someone on a college board." He winked. "If you know what I mean."

"Thanks, man. I will."

Arkady hung around while Vic served the lunch crowd. A little after noon, Yelena came in for her usual salad. She sat at Arkady's table with a short nod. "I tell you, this country is going to the dogs. If things continue like this, I'll actually be better off where I came from." Like Vic, she spoke Russian with him.

"Trouble?"

"Fucking spray-painting on my wall. 'Russki go home.' They like the jobs I offer and the taxes I pay just fine, though."

"That sucks."

"No shit. Now I'm going to have to put cameras up, or something." Her titanium facade cracked, and for a second she looked scared. "Shit." Then the crack disappeared again. "If I catch that son of a bitch, he'll volunteer in a refugee center when I'm done with him."

Arkady didn't doubt it.

They went on to bitch about the weather for a few minutes, before what she'd said earlier clicked in Arkady's brain. "About those cameras: do you have your own security people?"

She shook her head. "Not worth it. There's a service I'll call." Her eyes narrowed. "Why?"

"No, if you have someone . . ."

"I'm not saying there's no room for improvement."

"I might have just the guy to help improve your security, but I'll have to talk to him first. If you're both interested, he could call you?"

"I never say no to an offer I haven't heard yet."

Arkady laughed. "Fair enough."

He hung around after Yelena had left, to meet Maya, and schedule a first lesson. He suddenly couldn't wait to get back and tell Jason about what could be a first step in a new direction for him.

On the drive back though, doubt crept in. What if Jason didn't see it as a chance so much than as an intrusion? It wasn't, after all, any of Arkady's business whether he was happy in his job or not.

Arkady picked up a couple of subs and a six-pack on the way home, then installed himself on the couch and flipped through the TV channels. He laughed out loud when he came across a live snooker competition, and started watching it with amused desperation.

Thankfully Jason came home not too much later, and Arkady turned the TV off before his boredom could be noted or commented on.

There was always a strong urge to kiss Jason when he came in, but in light of their no-strings arrangement, that felt entirely too domestic. "There's food and beer," he said instead.

"Lifesaver." Jason always worked long days, and today he looked every minute of it.

"And we have a biometrics appointment for the first week of September," Arkady said on the way to the kitchen; he pointed at the mail on the table.

Jason glanced at it, but went over to the sink to wash his hands. "Excellent. Where?"

"Seattle."

"Crap. I'd been hoping it would be closer. I'll have to take the whole day off, then." His shoulders slumped; he sounded dead tired.

"A day off here and there'll do you good. You work way too many hours."

"Yeah." Jason's voice was dripping with sarcasm. "Staring at a TV screen all day really takes it out of you."

Arkady wasn't sure which of them he was talking about, but he couldn't completely keep the edge out of his voice when he said, "Believe me, I'd rather start working today than tomorrow."

Jason turned, towel in hand. "Shit. I didn't mean you. That came out wrong."

"At least your staring at the screen serves a purpose and pays the bills." Arkady popped open two beers and handed Jason one.

"I guess." Unwrapping the sub, Jason added, "Sauerkraut? How'd you know?"

"You seem like a Reuben kinda guy."

They started eating in silence. Arkady mentally kicked himself into action. It was now or never. "I went into Port Angeles today and ran into someone I know. She needs security advice on her office building, so I said I'd talk to you."

"Did you, now?"

That didn't sound too promising. "I'm not sure it'll pay anything, but if Yelena likes what you have to say, I am sure she'll find a way to show her gratitude. She's tough, but fair."

"Is that so?"

"Yeah." Damn Jason and his measured reactions. "I also told Vic I'd tutor his daughter in English." When Jason's eyebrow shot up, he added. "Not for money. Just a favor. It'll get my ass off your couch. For a couple afternoons per week, anyway."

Jason bit into his sub and chewed. Not the slightest clue in his face as to what he was thinking.

Now was probably a good time to shut up, but Jason's nonreactions were compelling. Like Arkady needed to break through somehow, needed to keep talking.

He pulled the biometrics letter toward himself. "We could visit Lily. Since we have to drive to Seattle anyway. Two birds with one—"

"Stop."

"Huh?"

Jason had put the rest of his sub back on the wrapping paper. "Stop trying to run my life."

"I wasn't— Look, all I want is to pull my weight. You don't want me to start fixing up the house? Fine. But you hate your job. At least let me help with that."

"Why?"

"Because I fucking can."

Jason picked his sub back up. "No, you can't." He took a quick, vicious bite; the first tiny sign of anger Arkady had seen. "You keep telling me I can be a security adviser," Jason said thickly. "But I wouldn't even know where to start."

"Oh, for fuck's sake, Jay—"

"Don't call me that." Jason looked as if Arkady had slapped him.

"What? Why?"

"Don't like it." It was obviously not that simple, but asking more questions wouldn't help.

"Okay. Fine. I won't. Seriously, though. At least check over Yelena's office building. Tell her what you see."

"Not a talker. You might have noticed."

Arkady stared at him. "Now you're just being pigheaded."

Jason shoved the last piece of bread in his mouth, not looking at him.

And suddenly Arkady understood. "You're scared."

For a moment Jason stared at the table, then he did look up. "Well, I'm not quitting my job on the off-chance of making it freelance."

"No one's asking you to. Do it on your day off. If nothing comes of it, you've lost a day you might otherwise have spent shooting at chestnuts. And if it does, start slow, cut down half a shift, take on a job here or there, see how you like it."

"Have to check my contract. Competition clause."

Arkady let out a sigh and took a long swig of his beer. This was like fighting windmills. "I guess you do. You have it here? Your contract?"

"Office."

"I give up."

"And we're not visiting Lily. Not together."

That came out of left field, and it hurt, especially that tacked on *Not together.*

"What'd I do now?"

Jason shook his head. "Nothing. But she already likes you. She'll expect you to be around. To come visit more often. And you'll likely be gone before Christmas. No need to make it hurt more than it already will."

Talking of hurt. So close to the first blow, the impact of the second took Arkady's breath away.

"Okay," he croaked. "You're right. I hadn't thought of that." Probably because he'd been trying so hard not to think of never seeing Lily again. Of eventually never seeing Jason again. *Before Christmas.* That was only four months away. Had he complained earlier about things not moving along fast enough? Well, he'd changed his mind. Not that it made a damned difference either way.

Jason went upstairs to clean up and take care of his leg, and Arkady straightened out the kitchen. There wasn't a lot to straighten; they barely used it. Taking in the cold stove, the torn walls and broken floor, staring the life they were living here in the face—fuck buddies—he understood with a sudden harsh clarity what Jason meant when he said this house was not a home.

"You coming to bed?" Jason called from upstairs.

"Go ahead, I'm not tired yet. I'll watch TV for a while."

Truth was, he couldn't face going upstairs and pretending that all he wanted from Jason was some dick. The *at least he'd have that* reasoning didn't work tonight. If only he could leave now, cut all ties, and never look back. Start something real with someone else. But he couldn't. Not yet. Maybe not ever. Because when he tried to imagine a relationship with someone else—someone not Jason—all he could come up with was a big fat blank.

In any case, he couldn't leave before the little plastic card came in the mail. And even then, he'd still have to list this as his address for the next two years, would have to come by to get his mail. Why had this seemed like a good idea again?

Because if not for this, you'd have a lifetime instead of two years of heartache, Izmaylov, so quit your whining.

He fell asleep on the couch and woke up, half-frozen, to the smell of coffee and Jason draping a blanket over him. He didn't move. What would he have said? *Good morning, love?*

For the next week, they tacitly kept away from each other. Arkady spent his days in Port Angeles and his nights on the couch, and Jason didn't comment. He also didn't ask again, whether Arkady would come up to bed.

Well, Arkady didn't want him to. He didn't want to explain what he was doing, or have to find another pathetic excuse. But damn, the disappointment was hard to wrestle down. He told himself a million times that hope without a chance was worse than no hope at all, and yet he woke up at fuck-thirty one night from fitful, restless sleep, thinking someone was pulling the blanket up around his shoulders, only to find the damned thing tangled between his ankles.

He didn't need this. What he needed was to get out of here, away from Jason, his couch, his naked, powerful shoulders in the morning, but most of all, away from those fucking tender little gestures that didn't mean a fucking thing.

He folded up his blankets, and was halfway through collecting his few possessions when it hit him that this was it. He wasn't coming back. Not to spend the night, anyway. Jason's paranoia about someone checking up on them be damned. No one was checking, because no one fucking cared, did they? He threw a glance up the stairs, then decided against getting his stuff from the bathroom. Soldiers were light sleepers when it came to unusual noises, and Arkady could get a toothbrush and a razor anywhere. A few bucks were a negligible price to pay for avoiding those searching eyes, and the tempting heartache that was Jason Cooley half-naked on the landing.

He left his keys on the kitchen table, then, trying not to be a dick, scribbled, *I'll be careful not to jeopardize the mission; just need a bit of space*, on a piece of printer paper, and shoved it underneath the keys.

He stubbornly refused to glance up the stairs again as he grabbed his gear and headed out to the car.

He didn't have a plan about where he was going, but when he found himself on the familiar road to Port Angeles, he didn't turn around. Tasha's would have been the more obvious place to go to, but that was another discussion he didn't need, another set of questions he didn't have answers for. Plus, Tasha had Anna, and while Arkady wished them all the happiness in the world, he couldn't bear being around a happy couple just now.

Suspended on the dark road, coming from nowhere, going nowhere, he wasn't sure whether he'd woken up at all. Had he really left Jason's house? Had he left Russia? What was real, and what was a dream? A light drizzle started to cover his windshield, giving the oncoming headlights a glaring halo. Blinding, straight in his face. He jerked the steering wheel to the right and hit the brakes, then stutter braking when the car started to skid. He didn't crash, but having overcompensated to the right, ended up on the grassy shoulder of the road, destroying a few ferns and low bushes in the process. God, he was so tired. Of everything.

He woke up to the buzzing of his phone in his pocket. He tried to fish it out, but he was trapped.

Seat belt. *What?* He couldn't get his brain in gear, but he did manage to unbuckle and fumble his phone out of his pocket.

"*Da?*"

"Where are you?" Jason asked.

Arkady flipped a mental switch to English, but that didn't provide an answer. "Are you checking up on me?" he asked back, mainly to buy himself some time.

"Just making sure you're not driving after getting plastered in some bar."

"Why would I— You *are* checking up on me."

There was a long pause on the other end, which gave Arkady a chance to check that he was in a car, and that it was dark outside. *Had* he been driving drunk?

"You didn't have to leave the key," Jason said.

With that Arkady's brain fired back up, and he knew where he was. Well, roughly. The clock on his phone read 4:12. Jason must have just gotten up.

"Wasn't sure whether you wanted me to hang on to it," Arkady said. Fuck, he had no idea what he was expected to say, or where he was going from here.

"The wedding planner?" Jason said.

"Huh?" It was like they were in one of those pretentious, postmodern plays, where nothing made sense. "What about the wedding planner?"

"Grigory? Is that where you are?"

"The fuck? Why the hell would I be at a wedding planner's? Are you on drugs?"

There was a brief silence, then Jason laughed. "Haven't even had coffee yet. Be careful, okay?" With that he disconnected.

Slowly Arkady let his hand sink, then he sat staring at his phone screen. There was no way he was going to make sense of that conversation, was there? Had Jason's laugh sounded relieved? And why would he want Arkady to keep the key? Oh, right, the mission— it'd look funny if Arkady rang the bell at the house he supposedly lived in; was that it?

Fuck, he so didn't have any of the answers tonight. He knew only two things with certainty: leaving in the middle of the night had been a stupid idea, and leaving had been his only option.

With an exasperated headshake, he shoved the phone back into his pocket, then reached for the key in the ignition. He turned it with some trepidation, but the engine started without any problems. Thank God for small favors.

It was still dark by the time he pulled into the parking lot behind Vic's, but dawn was creeping into the sky.

He waited until the coffee shop opened, then gave it another half hour, until there was a good breakfast crowd inside. The busier Vic was, the less time he'd have for chitchat and questions. He did actually give Arkady the raised-eyebrow treatment, but didn't say anything beyond good morning when it was Arkady's turn in the line to get his coffee and breakfast sandwich. Good thing it was one of the days he taught Maya, so at least he had that excuse, though it didn't explain why he was showing up here first thing in the morning.

By the time Vic came over to his table around eleven, Arkady had read his way through half the papers lying around.

"Find something interesting?" Vic nodded at the paper.

"Murder, mayhem, the usual," Arkady quipped. Then, to head off any deeper questions he added, "Also, I'm bored. What else is new?"

Vic wasn't buying it, though. "Too bored for sleep?" He pulled up a chair. "I have prep to do before I open, I get up early." With a nod toward the parking lot, he added. "Saw you pull in."

Arkady shrugged. "Fidgets, I guess."

Vic stared at him for what seemed like forever, before giving a brief nod and returning to work. Giving Arkady space he didn't want but needed to keep.

Arkady spent the day like that, between coffee, and magazines, and Vic's food, only leaving for a while when it was time for Maya's lessons.

He left for good a few minutes before closing, so Vic wouldn't think he had nowhere else to go. But then he sat undecided behind the wheel of his car. If he moved it to street parking, a cop was sure to find him sleeping in it, if he stayed here, Vic would know it. He pulled his phone out and started to search for motels, though he could ill afford the expense.

He was still checking when Vic knocked on his window. For a heartbeat Arkady was tempted to ignore him, then he rolled down the glass.

"Care to come up and share a beer with me?" Vic asked, then added before Arkady could say no, "Or do you prefer your solitary car-lot glory?"

Arkady huffed a laugh. He was trying to phrase a polite decline, when suddenly he couldn't remember why. Because he could really use the comfort and support Vic was offering. It wasn't the same as being surrounded by a large family, but it was closer than *solitary glory*.

Still . . . "No questions," he growled as he got out of the car. "Just beer."

Vic nodded. And he stuck to it, through three beers and beyond. Arkady relished simply having him around, the silent company of a sympathetic human being.

Finishing his beer, Vic said, "I've got to crash. Couch is yours, if you want it."

He didn't ask Arkady to decide, didn't hang around for an answer.

After he'd left, Arkady checked his phone. Jason would be home by now, even with his extra shift. There was no message, though. Well, what had he expected? He tried to tell himself that it was better this way, easier, less painful. He'd left to get away from the pain. So, why then was there still pain, why the disappointment? It was over; this would be so much easier if his heart could just accept that and move on. Find someone else, someone without commitment issues. It wouldn't be long now until he got his green card. That was the part he had to take on faith, because if he didn't believe that, then everything would fall apart. He'd get his green card and move to Port Angeles. There had to be people who were looking to share rent, some arrangement where he didn't need to put his name on a lease for the next two years. After that he could get a divorce. He'd find something, someone, a new life.

With that resolve firmly in mind, he attacked the newspapers again over coffee the next morning, this time, the ad section. Nothing jumped out at him, but it was too early anyway. He couldn't share rent until he had a job, and he couldn't get a job until he had his papers.

So he spent the day walking through Port Angeles, pretending he'd just moved here and was getting to know his new city. It wasn't bad at all, though there didn't seem to be a lot of cruising action. His phone mentioned one pickup bar, which was closed during the day, of course.

Arkady had dinner from a street cart, then a lonely beer at a pub. Hanging out at Vic's again seemed like too much of a pity party, though he'd left his car there, so Vic would know he was still around.

He went back to the gay bar about an hour after it opened, and while it wasn't quite humming on a weeknight, it wasn't empty either. His idea had been to have a drink and check things out in the process, but apparently that wasn't how it worked.

The second he walked in, heads turned. Some turned away again, but there was a number of definite winks, inviting smiles, a glass raised in a silent toast. He wasn't particularly shy about what he wanted, but he felt shy now. When he walked toward the bar, the grin of a man standing there suddenly seemed like a leer. It was followed by the crude invitation of a tongue flick. Kissing? That? Arkady's brain helpfully supplied the memory of Jason's slow, toe-curling kisses, and his stomach did a flip-flop. He almost hightailed it past the bar to throw up in the washroom, but beelining it there would look like he'd accepted the invite. With another dry heave, he turned on his heel and headed back out to the street, taking deep gulps of air as he walked, he didn't know where.

God, he'd really thought he could just walk in there and fuck Jason Cooley out of his system, hadn't he? Well, that had been spectacularly successful. A couple of passersby gave him a wide berth at his sudden humorless bark of laughter.

He needed to keep it together, but that unexpected flash of Jason's kisses had opened floodgates he didn't know how to close again. His chest, hell his whole skin, was too tight, every breath a painful drag, and there was a lump in his throat the size of Mother Russia. If he couldn't do this, if he couldn't walk away, what other option was there?

His phone buzzed. *No. Nonono.* He clamped a fist over his pocket and gritted his teeth, and after a while it stopped.

The street he'd turned into looked familiar; he'd circled back to Vic's without conscious navigation. The café as well as the apartment above were dark, but Vic had left a note under his wiper that the couch was his until further notice. *No questions.*

He'd also left the back door unlocked. So, Arkady made his way upstairs in the dark and crashed on the couch again, eons farther away from a solution than he had been the night before.

Vic woke him up the next morning before heading downstairs. "Maya won't be up for another hour," he said. "Shower's that way. You need it."

Arkady nodded, no surprise there.

But Vic wasn't done. "I've seen you guys together, Jason and you; I saw you at your wedding. And I can't imagine a lot of reasons why you wouldn't fight like hell to keep what you have. That's not a question. If you don't want to talk about it, that's your choice. But at least think about it."

Arkady almost laughed. Like he'd done anything else these past seventy-two hours, the past weeks even. Maybe ever since he'd met Jason at the airport.

But all he said was, "Thanks."

Vic was right: he didn't want to talk about it. And what would he have said? That Vic was wrong? That Jason and Arkady had played them all? The small voice inside that whispered, *What if he isn't wrong?* was hard to ignore, though. Hope was a tough little bitch to kill. He'd have to try harder. Because if Vic was right, if Jason did care, then why the fuck wouldn't he just say so? He held all the cards.

Arkady headed to the shower, managed to avoid dousing himself with green apple shampoo at the last second, and came back to the buzzing of his phone.

His first thought was Jason, and he wanted to kick himself, because why would Jason call him? It was probably Tasha.

It *was* Jason. "Hey."

The quiet, single-syllable rumble sent goose bumps skittering up Arkady's arms. "Hey."

"Just wanted to make sure you haven't forgotten our appointment," Jason said.

Arkady's heart thudded one loud *Fuck!* against his ribs. "Course not," he lied. The biometrics appointment. Tomorrow's biometrics appointment. "What time do you want to leave? I can come and get you. No use taking two cars." He was grateful for how smooth he was able to keep his voice. If one discounted the thudding heartbeat underneath, that was.

"We shouldn't show up in different cars anyway," Jason said immediately. "Are you at Natalya's?" That sounded careful, as if he were expecting to be told to mind his own business.

"Right now? No, I'm at Vic's. It's one of Maya's lesson days." It wasn't a lie, but why was he phrasing that as if he'd just gotten here? It was none of Jason's business where he spent his nights, or stood half-naked in the living room with water dripping out of his hair. Especially since it wasn't what Jason would be thinking at all.

Arkady became suddenly aware of the prolonged silence on the other end and added, "Why?"

"I thought, since we have to leave early tomorrow, you might want to crash here tonight, give you an hour or so more sleep than if you'd have to drive over in the morning." Before Arkady could say anything, he added quickly, "Or I could pick you up."

"No, it's okay, I'll be there. It does make sense to stay at your place." It did, didn't it? Arkady wasn't just telling himself that because he didn't want Jason to know where he was spending his nights? No, because *that* would *not* make any sense.

"I'll leave the porch light on." Jason paused as if he was going to say something else, but merely added, "See you tomorrow, then."

And Arkady's stupid heart did a double thud at that. *Shut up!*

He made it through the day on autopilot, his whole being focused on the evening, on returning to a place that wasn't even home, no matter how many times he told himself to grow up, or how scathingly his inner voice poked fun at his baseless hopes. Nothing would happen—he would sleep on the couch, they'd drive to Seattle and back, and that was all there was to it. Hell, he didn't want anything to happen. That was precisely why he'd left in the first place.

He was still arguing with himself when he pulled into the driveway behind Jason's ancient Camry just after nine. Late enough not to have to kill an agonizing evening, but not so late that he'd be kicking Jason out of bed.

Arkady didn't get a chance to ring the bell; Jason must've heard the car. He looked tired, even in the less-than-stellar light.

"You work too much."

Jason opened his mouth as if to say something in return, but then shrugged and made room for Arkady to come inside.

The place looked exactly the same. *You've been gone three days, hotshot.* It felt much longer than that.

Jason had already pulled out the couch and put a sheet, pillow, and blanket on it. Arkady couldn't decide if he was relieved or disappointed that there was no doubt about where he'd be sleeping tonight. God, he was messed up.

"Want a beer?" Jason asked.

"Naw, we'll be up early. I think I'm just gonna crash."

Again Jason looked as if he was going to comment, and again he shrugged and gave Arkady space.

"Good night, then," he said over his shoulder, already halfway up the stairs.

"Good night."

While Jason was in the bathroom, Arkady did a load of laundry, then went to brush his teeth, carefully listening for any potential doors opening, before he crawled under his blanket. There was no reason why he should, but he felt better than he had in days and was out like a light as soon as his head hit the pillow.

The next day they took the rental car, which was newer and more comfortable than Jason's old Camry, and shared the driving. Jason drove down to Seattle, because he was used to being awake in the morning, and Arkady drove back.

Six hours in the car, and an hour of waiting for an appointment that had taken all of five minutes, and the silence between them had been deafening all day. They were almost home when, out of nowhere, halfway between Sequim and Port Angeles, Jason asked, "Want to stop in Port Angeles?" He had his eyes closed and his head against the backrest.

Arkady'd thought he was asleep. "I hadn't planned on it, but I can if you want me to. Bathroom break?"

"No, I'm good. That woman, Yelena? You think she's hired someone else by now?"

Arkady threw a glance to his right, but Jason's eyes were still closed. "Come again?"

"I know it's a long shot, but since we're here, and I already took the day off anyway..."

For a brief satisfying moment, Arkady wanted to tell him to go fuck himself. Then hope raised its shiny little head. Was this a peace offering? *For what, Izmaylov? You haven't been fighting.*

Most likely Jason had simply had enough time to get over his stage fright. Or something had pissed him off enough at work to take desperate measures.

"I guess we'll see," was all Arkady said. He pulled up *Vanin Enterprises* on the GPS, because he usually came into town from the other side, and he didn't feel like getting lost after all the driving they'd already done today.

He called Yelena on his mobile from the visitor parking spot in front of the building instead of walking in unannounced. A polite pretense at not barging in on her at the end of the work day. She was still in, though, and invited them upstairs.

Jason dug his aviator shades out of the glove compartment and hid his eyes behind them. In his black jeans and T-shirt, he looked dangerously competent, as if he could take on anyone and anything and waste them with a flick of his wrist.

Yelena's office was on the fifth floor, but Jason chose the stairs over the elevator and had a peek into every hallway on their way up.

"You're lucky," Yelena said after Arkady had introduced them. "I was just about to leave."

"My fault." Jason held out his hand, and she shook it. "I wasn't sure what time we'd be back from Seattle."

Her eyebrow shot up, and Arkady didn't blame her. He hadn't expected Jason's matter-of-fact, no apologies approach either.

"Do you find the lights too bright, Mr. Cooley?" she asked with a nod at his sunglasses.

"I'm fine, but thanks for asking." He gave her a shark grin, and the shades stayed on.

This was shaping up like an old-school showdown. Too bad Arkady didn't have any popcorn. He'd never seen Jason like this and was thoroughly intrigued.

Yelena walked around Jason, looking him up and down. He could have been a structural support in her office for all the heed he paid her.

"So you're the one-glance wonder," she finally said.

"Ma'am?"

"Arkady promised you could tell what was wrong with my security at a glance."

Jason half turned and threw Arkady a look over the top of his glasses that sent shivers all the way down into Arkady's toes. "How bold."

"I'm willing to let it slide," Yelena said. "Marketing is about hyperbole, after all, isn't it?"

Jason ignored her reply. "The security cam overlooking your visitor parking is fake. There's a fence on the west side that provides easy access to the annex roof, and thus to open windows. Someone propped the fire escape door to the back open while taking a smoking break, then walked away around the corner so the smoke wouldn't drift inside." Jason gave her the same over-the-rims look he'd given Arkady. "Did they also disable the alarm, or are the fire escapes not provided with one?"

"You noticed all that just getting out of your car and walking up the stairs?"

He took his shades off and slid one of the arms into the neck opening of his T-shirt, so they'd stay there. "That's my job. This was the free sample. For a full inspection and report, I need unhindered access to the building for twenty-four hours. Supervised will be fine. Preferred, in fact."

She nodded and thought for a moment. "You can provide advice about any equipment we might need?"

"Affirmative."

She gave him a speculative look. "You're not afraid of me, Mr. Cooley, are you?"

"No, ma'am."

She laughed and held out a card. "I like that. Very well, why don't you send me an estimate and we'll go from there."

"Yes, ma'am. Thank you."

They said their goodbyes and left. This time Jason didn't insist on taking the stairs, so they took the elevator down. Arkady studied him bemused. So that, apparently, was the soldier Jason Cooley, whatever his rank had been when he got out. *Holy shit.* "I take it back, what I said earlier about you being scared."

Jason didn't answer, but after a moment he held out his hand, palm down. It was shaking.

Arkady laughed. "Remind me to never, ever play poker with you."

They didn't talk in the car, but now the silence was different. The strain had gone out of it. Which wasn't to say there was no tension between them, but it was the kind generated by aviator shades, and biceps straining T-shirt sleeves, and the hard edge of a thigh muscle in black jeans. How the hell he was supposed to stay away from that, Arkady had no idea.

He tried to keep his eyes on the road and his mind on the traffic. But by the time they made it home, his own jeans were fitting uncomfortably tight in the inseam.

The tiny hallway always felt crowded when they both got in the door together, but lately the damned thing seemed to be getting even smaller.

Arkady squeezed his way through into the living room with a deep breath. He was intensely aware of every inch of skin under his clothes.

Jason made a beeline for the stairs. Shower? Hardly bed—it wasn't even seven. But then he stopped in the middle of the room without turning. "Uhm."

Arkady didn't have the foggiest idea what he was working himself up to say, so he just waited.

When Jason finally did turn, he threw a long look at the couch, then a quick one at Arkady, before seemingly getting lost in a study of the bare floor. "I was thinking . . ." He made a vague gesture toward the stairs.

Arkady held his breath. "You want me to come upstairs?" God, he wanted to. Reason be damned.

Now Jason did look at him; there was a deep V between his brows. "Only if you want to." His voice sounded way more gravelly than usual.

Arkady almost rolled his eyes. "Why would I ask if I didn't want to?"

Jason shrugged. "Polite?"

A short laugh escaped Arkady. He shook his head and closed the distance between them. "You ask if someone wants salt to be polite, not if they want to be fucked."

"You didn't ask—"

"Yes. As a matter of fact I did." He cupped both hands around Jason's neck. Fuck, the man was tense. "Hell yeah, I want to come upstairs with you."

Jason made a strained sound somewhere in his chest, then wrapped Arkady in a bear hug. "I thought you didn't want me anymore," he mumbled against Arkady's neck.

"Yeah, like that's going to happen," Arkady said under his breath. It would make things so much easier. To Jason he said, "Go on, lead the way." He'd never get tired of watching Jason's ass. Or of marveling how he couldn't tell that Jason was walking with an artificial leg. Even up the stairs.

At the same time, he had a lump in his throat; there was a strangely vulnerable mood between them. As if they had rubbed each other raw and were both aware of it.

In the bedroom, Jason stopped again as if undecided what to do next. Arkady had never seen him so insecure.

"Are you sure you want me here?" Arkady asked.

"Yes." No hesitation there.

"Then what's going on?"

Jason turned to him and laid a hand against his cheek, tracing the cheekbone with his thumb.

Jesus, God.

"You're so . . ." Jason gestured at Arkady's body, top to bottom to top. "I have no idea why you want me."

"Seriously?"

Jason turned away from him. "I'm not exactly a prize," he mumbled.

Arkady stood stunned into silence for a couple of seconds, then he let out his disbelief in a barked laugh. "Man, you're messed up." Time to lock his own pains and longings away and take care of Jason's glaring needs for a bit.

"I think you need some mirror therapy for your full body to tell your brain what is actually there." He took Jason by the shoulders and turned him toward the mirrored closet door. "'I will give out divers schedules of your beauty,'" he misquoted, standing behind Jason. "'Item, two lips that leave me anything but indifferent; item, two hazel eyes with lids to them'. Damn, I can't remember how it goes on. Doesn't matter, though." He grabbed the hem of Jason's T-shirt and pulled it up and over his head when Jason obediently raised his arms.

Arkady whistled softly through his teeth. "Now, will you look at that." He skimmed the back of his fingers along Jason's neck and kissed it, then ran both palms over Jason's shoulders. "That column of a neck, those damn deltoids, that fucking arm porn that makes my throat so dry I can't swallow anymore."

Jason stood as still as a statue; only his eyes followed Arkady's hands.

"And will you look at those pecs?" Arkady raked his fingernails across Jason's nipples and listened to the short gasp that elicited. God, he'd missed the man.

"That six-pack."

Jason's abdominal muscles spasmed when Arkady lightly ran his fingers across them.

Arkady opened the button on Jason's jeans and pulled down the zipper, then, with a swift movement, stripped both jeans and briefs down to his ankles.

Jason's fingers twitched as if he was going to hold on to his pants, but he didn't.

"That ass? Jesus, God, that ass!" Arkady grabbed Jason's hips and pressed his hard-on against said ass, then let his hands roam down and inward. "These? I believe the English vernacular is 'cum gutters'? I want to lick them."

A tremor ran through Jason's body, and his dick started to rise like a vehicle barrier.

"I dream of that dick fucking me flat against the wall," Arkady whispered into his ear.

"Christ, man. You're killing me," Jason hissed back.

"Like. Right now." Arkady couldn't suppress a grin.

Jason promptly bent to take his shoes off and to get rid of the cloth pile around his ankles, and Arkady quickly stripped as well, then dove across the bed to the drawer that held condoms and lube.

Coming back, he couldn't help a slap across Jason's bare ass. It was too inviting.

"Watch it," Jason growled. He drummed his fingers against the black sleeve covering his knee. "You, uhm, want me to keep this on?" His eyes met Arkady's in the mirror, trepidation in their depths.

"Your call."

When Jason didn't move, Arkady laid his forehead against Jason's neck. "Listen, I can only imagine what's going on inside you, and probably badly at that. And I have no clue what you need to hear from me at this moment. So all I can give you is my take on this: As far as I'm concerned that prosthesis is just a tool. Or maybe not 'just'; it's a medical engineering feat. Still a tool, though. An aid. Like glasses." He paused, then drawled, butchering the accent, "And frankly, my dear, I don't give a damn if you keep your glasses on in bed or not."

Jason huffed a laugh.

"But," Arkady went on, "I'm down with whatever helps me get fucked against that wall."

CHAPTER ELEVEN

Jason took the lube and condoms Arkady held out, then watched him brace against the wall.

He had a lump in his throat the size of Mount Olympus. That Arkady, buck-naked and obviously turned on as hell had taken the time—again—to acknowledge Jason's problem, had not laughed at it, and still managed to put it in some kind of perspective, that was shifting something heavy in Jason's chest, something he hadn't been all that aware of, because he was so used to its weight.

He cleared his throat and gave one of the condoms back. "You better put that on. I'm not planning on repainting that wall anytime soon."

Arkady laughed. "Good point. Because I plan on enjoying this to the hilt." He winked outrageously at his own pun, which looked so funny on his made-for-melancholy face that Jason, too, had to laugh.

Arkady rolled the condom on, inhaling sharply when he touched himself, then put both hands up against the wall again. On edge, then. Good to know.

God, he was gorgeous. Jason let his hands roam all over Arkady's back, his ass, his legs; leaned in to him and pressed kisses into his hair and against his neck and shoulders.

Arkady's breath quickened. "I don't have all day, you know."

"Oh, yes, you do." Damn, Jason was glad he'd kept the prosthesis on. It might not be the most romantic look in the world, but it gave him so much more control than lying on the bed, and he intended to use that control to its full capacity.

Arkady hissed something in Russian that sounded like a curse. Jason smiled. He couldn't remember having felt this amazing in ages.

He warmed a generous amount of lube in his hand, then massaged it into Arkady's ass.

"Yes, please. Finally," Arkady groaned.

Jason lined his dick up and started pushing, very slowly, until he felt resistance. He rested his chin on Arkady's shoulder and whispered, "This what you want?"

"Yes. Now!"

Jason gently bit his ear and gave him another inch.

"Jason, I swear to God—"

"You realize that the more you swear at me, the slower I'll go, right?"

"Pizd— Gawd!" Arkady shut up, and for a second Jason feared he'd explode with the effort to relax, then he hung his head and the tension went out of his shoulders with a long exhale.

"I knew you could do it."

Whatever Arkady might have answered was lost in his harsh gasp when Jason slammed all the way home.

"Too much?"

"Perfect." It came out as a huff of air.

Jason pulled back slowly, then slammed forward again.

A soft whimper came from Arkady that sounded desperate for more rather than hurt, so Jason kept up his rhythm like that for a while. The slow pullback helped him to hold his own. He didn't want to come just yet, wanted to stay in this moment forever: Arkady's long, curved back in front of him, arms trembling with the effort to hold himself up. Trusting him, wanting him, like, really, seriously wanting him.

He'd looked at Jason in the mirror and talked of beauty. The flashback of Arkady caressing the different parts of his body with hands and words pushed Jason off his plateau, and he felt himself speeding up. He wouldn't be able to hold back much longer. But then, Arkady had wanted to be flat against the wall hadn't he? Well, that could be arranged.

One hand securely on Arkady's chest, Jason drove his body forward, again and again, the friction, the heat between them, the sounds Arkady made, nearly annihilating him, until, with a soft *oof,* Arkady's arms gave, and he did indeed end up flat against the wall.

A shudder like an earthquake ran through his body, his ass cheeks clenched, and like a flame traveling up a fuse, the tremor continued through Jason's body, spread into side quakes, and finally shook loose his own orgasm, a seismic event off any scale he'd previously established, that buried sight, sound, and time.

When his ears finally worked again, all he could hear was the *boom, boom* of his own heartbeat in his ears. His skin was slick against Arkady's back, the scent of Arkady's sweat and shampoo in his nose, Arkady's hair damp against his face.

He took in a big gulp of air and slowly straightened up, not quite trusting his muscles to do their job. He winced when he pulled out, too tender now for the tight friction, even if it was only for a second.

Arkady slumped in his arms and unable to get a grip on his sweat-slick skin, Jason had to gently let him slide to the floor.

He went into the bathroom for one of the large towels, wrapped Arkady up in that, and moved him over to the bed. "Stay," Arkady murmured.

"Don't worry. I'm not going anywhere."

Jason removed the prosthesis and checked the stump, deciding it would survive for one night without the usual shower. Then he pulled the cover over both of them, and Arkady's body against his, still back to chest. That way he could bury his face in those blond curls, feel Arkady's heartbeat slow down against his palm and listen to his breathing evening out into sleep.

Jason woke from a deep sleep at two in the morning and then drifted between sleep and waking until four, when he had to get up. He felt suspended somehow, as if given a reprieve from a breaking and broken world to a place where he could be whole.

He turned the alarm off before it could ring, so it wouldn't wake Arkady, then silently collected his stuff and snuck into the bathroom. But when he came back out, there was a light on in the kitchen and the sounds of water running and cabinet doors being opened and closed.

He came downstairs to the coffee already brewing and Arkady busy in front of a pile of bread, making sandwiches. In jeans, and nothing else. Hair like a halo around his head. *Sweet Lord.*

Arkady turned when Jason walked in, and wrapped his arms around Jason's neck, pulling him into a soft, languid kiss. "Good morning."

"Yeah," Jason breathed. "No shit it is." He pointed at the sandwiches. "Plans for the day?"

"Oh, those are for you. Cheese with mayo and lettuce, ham with mustard and pickle, one PBJ, and one PB banana, right?"

Jason swallowed hard. "Look at you, paying attention," he said. Because there were no adequate words for what was going on inside him. In his world people didn't kiss in kitchens. And they sure as hell didn't make him sandwiches before dawn. He poured himself a mug of coffee. He needed it.

Arkady threw him a puzzled glance. "I— If you're not okay with this—"

"No. No, I am. I'm absolutely okay with it. It's— You are—" *Breathe, Cooley. Don't forget to breathe.* "Thank you." To figure out what he really wanted to say, he had to figure out what to think, which meant he had to figure out what was going on here. *Shouldn't take more than a few lifetimes. Fuck buddies, right?*

Arkady still seemed dubious, so Jason said over the rim of his mug. "I swear, I'm okay. I just don't know what to say. I'm not used to . . ." He threw a vague wave at Arkady and the food on the counter.

The corner of Arkady's mouth twitched; Jason expected a quip, but then Arkady seemed to reconsider, and held his peace. Good thing, because Jason didn't think he could have dealt with sarcasm or teasing right now. He still felt weird. Powerful and fragile at the same time, and raw and open. He didn't know which way he could move without cracking something, and he had no idea why. Arkady had left because he'd needed space, he'd come back for a fuck, they'd fucked and Arkady'd made sandwiches. Nothing cosmic had happened. Things hadn't really changed.

Despite that, his weird mood held over the next few weeks. It mellowed to something slightly less raw, but it didn't disappear, and Arkady seemed to feel it too. They were dancing around each other with a strange tenderness of words and gestures and light, reassuring touches rather than sex. Though there was that too.

Work-wise, Jason agonized over what price to quote Yelena for the consult, and in the end went with what he was making per hour right now. Arkady thought it was too low, but told him to go with what he was comfortable with. Yelena sent him back an immediate *Yes!* Over all, the whole process, down to the actual writing of the report, was way less agonizing than he had imagined. He even felt like he was doing something worthwhile. Something he might want to do again. Maybe not immediately, but at some point, after the feeling of being new at this had lost its edge.

Near the end of October, the appointment for their interview appeared in the mail, and the mood between Arkady and him changed.

"Twenty-sixth October." Arkady slapped the letter against his thigh, brows drawn together, the envelope clearly forgotten in his other hand. "That's Wednesday already." He emitted a sudden nervous tension that Jason could feel radiating against his own skin, trying to worm its way under. He couldn't let it. This last test was mission critical. "Well, you know the color of my toothbrush," he drawled.

Arkady laughed. "And how you drink your coffee, and which side of the bed you sleep on." But the tension didn't leave his shoulders.

They'd downloaded truckloads of sample questions and had been going through them for weeks now. Plus Arkady did actually live here again. There'd been no more nights away, or keys left on the table. Hell, they slept in the same bed. Jason didn't see how this could possibly go wrong. Which was, of course, exactly the famous-last-words scenario he should guard against. But they had. To outward appearances at least, he didn't see how their lives could be any more intertwined than they already were. Not that he was an expert on relationships. He assumed that Arkady was way better at those than he was. And Arkady was nervous. Not good, that.

"Can I ask you something?" Arkady had gotten them both beers out of the fridge, and now stood staring at the door.

"Shoot."

"Why is Lily not in your life?"

Jason mentally tried to shift gears. "What do you mean 'why not'? Why do you think you're here?"

Arkady shook his head. "I'm not talking about money. I'm talking about actual contact, having her over, going to the zoo, that sort of thing. You haven't seen her since the wedding. I thought at first it might be about what you said, that she shouldn't get used to me, but that isn't it, is it? You haven't been to see her on your own either."

"I'm working a lot."

"Yeah, I know. But come on, how often have you seen her since she was born? Do I need one hand or two?"

"I fail to see how that's any of your business." The questions shouldn't have made Jason feel called out, much less cornered, because he had valid reasons for not elbowing into Lily's life. But they did, and his answer had been harsher than he'd intended.

But Arkady didn't back down. He wasn't looking at Jason, was still staring at the fridge door, at Lily's photo probably. "I just really need to know why. Not the 'I work hard, and it's a long drive' answer. The real reason. Please. It's important."

There were undertones here that went beyond what they were actually saying, but Jason couldn't put his finger on them. He shrugged. It was hard to put his reasons into so many words, no matter how much sense they made to him. "I don't want to get in the way," he finally said. "She's a smart kid. Like, seriously smart. And she has parents who love her. I don't have anything to add to that."

"You're wrong. In more ways than one. It takes a village to raise a child. How could she have too much love?"

Jason bristled at the *You're wrong*, but tried to keep it out of his voice. "Good intentions don't guarantee good outcomes."

"So you don't even try?"

He wouldn't be able to keep a lid on his temper much longer. He *was* trying, *his* way. And Arkady knew that. He shook his head; they were going around in circles. "You need to back off, buddy."

Arkady shrugged, or tried to. There was so much tension in his shoulders that it looked tortured. This wasn't about Lily at all, was it?

"What exactly are we arguing about?"

At that Arkady finally turned. "I'm not arguing. I'm just trying to figure out— Ah, hell, I'm probably kidding myself, and it's a moot point anyway." He looked disappointed and defeated now.

Jason had no idea how something nearly perfect had deteriorated so fast and so completely. He wasn't surprised though. That was exactly how life worked. Still, he tried one more time.

"It takes a lot of things to raise a child. Some people have it, and some people don't. All I'm saying is, those who don't, shouldn't raise children."

"And you think you don't?"

"I know I don't."

"I still think you're wrong," Arkady said softly. "But nothing I say will change your mind, will it?"

Jason's patience slipped. Arkady was getting a fucking green card out of their deal, and he'd made it amply clear that that, and nothing else, *was* the deal. Which didn't give him any fucking right to fuck with anybody's fucking feelings. "Why would you want to? Why the fuck do you even care?"

"Yeah, I'm asking myself that. I really shouldn't."

With that Arkady left. Not just the kitchen. He grabbed his fucking keys on the way out, and Jason heard his car engine start up outside, with no idea whether he'd come back this time, and out of fresh excuses to call him if he didn't. How could they feel so solid together, when whatever they had could break any second? *Because it's all in your head, Cooley. It'll break, and soon, because it's meant to. Because that's the plan, remember? Fuck!*

He kicked the trash can across the room in frustration, and nearly lost his balance. Great. For a second he'd forgotten about his leg. He hadn't thought that was possible. With a bark of laughter, he sank down on one of the kitchen chairs. *Good fight. Thanks for nothing.*

He nuked his dinner, and ate it in inglorious silence, wishing he'd never heard of Arkady Izmaylov.

Arkady came back a little after midnight, smelling of booze and cigarettes. He blinked when he saw Jason sitting on the couch with his laptop.

"What are you doing still up?" He was clearly trying hard not to slur his words. He looked around, then dropped his jacket where he was standing.

"Making sure you didn't wrap yourself around a tree. You shouldn't drink and drive."

"Don't tell me what to do." It didn't sound aggressive, though, but quiet, almost soothing. Like what he'd really wanted to say was, *Don't worry about me.*

Jason laughed. "Really? Well, look who's talking."

Arkady sat down next to him, and Jason immediately shoved his hands into his pockets. The heat between them never seemed to die, no matter what they were currently throwing at each other.

"I'm sorry," Arkady said. "I shouldn't have said anything. I guess it's just something I want so much that it's been bugging me. I can't understand it. But that's no excuse. I was way out of line, and I'm sorry."

Wait. What? Want what so much?

Before he could actually ask that question, Arkady leaned against him and rested his head on Jason's shoulder. "The world's a funny place," he said. "And not as in 'ha ha.'"

Jason gave up. He wrapped both arms around Arkady and pulled him close. "Half the time I don't know what you're talking about when you're sober; I'm not even going to try when you're drunk."

"It gives you all these amazing things, then takes them away again," Arkady said, snuggling his nose under Jason's chin.

"Now there's a truth."

"Never mind. Take me to bed."

"Want me to carry you up the stairs?"

Arkady sat up. "You couldn't. Could you?"

"Don't be so sure," Jason growled.

A shiver ran through Arkady's body. "Oh, hell, yeah."

Wednesday morning they dressed in business formals, tacitly shined shoes, and straightened each other's ties. Arkady recoiled when Jason asked him what he wanted for breakfast, and he only took one sip of coffee, then spit it into the sink.

"I'm okay," he said, when Jason half rose from his chair. "I just don't feel like eating."

"It'll all work out," Jason said. Did people say that as a prayer or a reassurance? Both?

"It better work out, because if not, I don't know what I'll do. I can't go back. Now less than ever."

"You won't have to." Prayer it was.

"I wish . . . it was already done."

It had sounded like he'd been about to say something else, but Jason didn't ask. He merely took the hint, ate his sandwich in two bites, and washed it down with the coffee. "Let's hit the road, then." He'd had to call in a few favors to get the day off on less than a week's notice, but hearing the reason, everyone had made an effort and wished them luck.

They were on their way to the car when the phone rang in the house. Arkady held up the key he'd just been about to put in his pocket. "I got it," he said, and went back inside when Jason shrugged.

Jason picked some fall leaves off the rental's wipers. He quite liked driving this car. He could use a new one himself, but that wasn't going to happen. Not until the Camry fell apart under him. In the meantime he'd enjoy this one. He got in, started the engine, and clicked through the radio stations until some folk rock came up. Then he drummed his fingers on the wheel. He was just about to go check, when Arkady came out of the house.

"Who was it?" Jason asked as Arkady folded himself into the seat.

"Kendra. Apparently 'that fool, Jason Cooley' sent her 'way more money than he can fucking afford.'" He tsked and shook his head. "You didn't send her all of it at once, did you?"

"No," Jason growled, as he started the car. "I knew she'd be suspicious. I just sent her the five grand for the application for now. For Lily's school," he added when Arkady's brows drew together. "What'd you tell her?"

"That you might have mentioned a bonus from work."

"Thanks."

Morning traffic was scant, rush hour hadn't started yet. Arkady threw him occasional sideways glances, until Jason finally asked, "Anything else?"

"Nope." Arkady grinned at him. "At least nothing that can't be summed up under 'that fool, Jason Cooley.'"

Jason grunted.

They made it to the interview with half an hour to spare. Jason got himself a coffee, while Arkady still didn't want any, then they went to find out where exactly they were supposed to go.

At a window marked *Registration*, they presented their letter and IDs.

The guy behind the glass took his sweet time studying both. "So, which one of you is the girl?" He was speaking into a microphone on his side, and the question echoed through the waiting room and made every head turn.

Jason straightened his shoulders and stuck his chin out. "Excuse me?"

Arkady laid a calming hand on his back.

But Mr. Sensitivity was laughing hard at his own joke and waved Jason's challenge aside. "Room 324. Elevator's on your left." He winked. "They have cameras in them."

Jason swallowed the *Fuck you* when he saw the warning on Arkady's face. "Seriously though," he said when they were out of hearing distance. "Was that guy for real?"

"Are you kidding me? That wasn't even worth the effort of raising an eyebrow. Shrug it off and move on."

"He shouldn't be allowed to get away with it."

Arkady barked a laugh. "You can come back here to pick that fight with him once we have what we want."

He was right, of course. But that didn't mean that Jason had to like it.

Room 324 was one door in a long row along a longer corridor. Chairs were placed against the wall opposite the door in groups of twos and threes. Jason checked his watch. Still ten minutes to go. He sat down and sipped his coffee, while Arkady prowled the corridor.

The door opened a few minutes later, when a couple in their forties left with encouraging nods to Jason, and goodbyes to the woman behind them holding the door. She was black, middle-aged, sporting a charcoal business suit and Josephine Baker hair without the squiggle. "Jason Cooley and Arkady Izmaylov?" she asked.

They shook hands, she introduced herself as Christine Bailey and offered two seats in front of her desk.

Jason surreptitiously stuck his cup under his chair.

They chatted for a bit about the weather, while Christine pulled their file up on her screen. Arkady was fidgeting beside him, so Jason laid a hand on his thigh in a silent attempt to calm him down. His fingers were squeezed in a hard grasp.

"So," Christine said. "Tell me about yourselves." She started with Jason. "How did you two meet?"

"Arkady's sister and I work together. I gave her a lift to the airport to pick him up."

"Love at first sight, then?"

"Well, it was *something* at first sight," Arkady said, looking at Jason like he was seeing *something* amazing.

"I was just the driver," Jason said. "But I knew I wanted to see him again." That part at least was the truth.

"Where was your first date?"

"In a pub," Arkady said. "Not that we called the first one a date. We were still figuring out the lay of the land."

"But the one after was also pub," Jason supplied helpfully. "And that one was most definitely a date."

"What was the best date you had?"

They looked at each other. They hadn't prepared for that question.

"The woods," Arkady said slowly. "I was thinking about how familiar the landscape was. How easily it could be home."

Jason hadn't known that, but it felt like the truth. It gave him goose bumps. He nodded. "Target practice." He turned to Christine. "It was a typical boys' day out." Looking back at Arkady he added, "But it turned surprisingly deep."

Arkady's throat moved as he swallowed; he squeezed Jason's hand.

"Who typically cooks the meals when you're home, Mr. Cooley?"

"Neither of us knows how to cook." Here they were on safe ground again. "The microwave is our friend. And I make a mean sandwich."

"And a good breakfast," Arkady added.

Jason hooked a thumb at him. "Arkady is the king of instant noodles."

Arkady burst out laughing. "Trust you to remember that."

She asked some more questions, about dates they'd had, their daily routines, how they spent weekends, while leafing through the documents they'd brought, and the wedding album Vic's daughter, Maya, had made for them.

"The little girl is a relative?" She pointed at a picture of Lily dancing with Arkady.

"My daughter." Jason had been sure she would ask about that.

Christine checked her screen. "Yes, I see here you mentioned a child. You didn't claim her as a dependent, though?"

"No. She lives with her mother and stepfather."

"When did your relationship with her mother end?"

"There was no relationship. No romantic one anyway. Kendra, Lily's mother, and I were schoolmates and friends. There was a party, drinks, then I got deployed. Kendra never gave me any indication that she wanted me in her life, and she got married soon after. And I was in the service, of course, then in the hospital, rehab, trying to get my life back together. Not a good space for a relationship."

"Did she know you're gay?"

"Bisexual. No, she didn't. Not back then. I didn't know either." He had to force himself not to look at Arkady. Christine gave him no indication whether she considered his answers sufficient. It made him nervous, and made it hard not to fidget, so he concentrated on his even breathing instead of her face.

She checked her screen again. "You've had quite the whirlwind romance. Who proposed?"

"I did," Arkady said. When she merely nodded expectantly, he added, "I'd bought the ring that morning and was going to wait until dinner that night." He turned to Jason. "But when I saw you at the studio, I couldn't wait. It was burning a hole in my pocket."

Another answer that gave Jason goose bumps. He was starting to feel decidedly off-kilter.

"Did it take you by surprise, Mr. Cooley?"

"A little." No use denying that. It must have been plain for anyone to see.

"Did you have doubts?"

"No."

"None? It wasn't a decision one makes every day." Was she trying to trap him? Voicing her doubt? Giving him rope to hang himself with?

"I'm used to making split decisions about life and death. And I know what I want." This time he couldn't keep himself from throwing a glance at Arkady. God, yes, he wanted that man. *Concentrate!*

"And have you talked about what you want? About the future? Do you know what Arkady wants?"

Jesus, fuck. He didn't have a clue, because there was no future. She'd caught him cold, and he was dead. They both were.

"Family!" he blurted out. He had no idea where the thought had come from, but he knew he was right. "It's a bit of a weird one, I know, with Lily already part of one family, but we're making it work." It sounded true. *Please, God, make her believe that.*

Christine gave another one of her noncommittal nods. "When did you know it was more than just 'something at first sight'?" she asked, coming back to Arkady's earlier answer.

"First date," Jason said. Sweat was pooling under his arms and at the small of his back. "The one that wasn't a date. Afterward there was a kiss in a doorway . . ." He stalled, suddenly unsure how much detail was appropriate.

"Sparks," Arkady added, uncharacteristically terse.

She typed briefly, then said to Arkady, "And what, aside from sparks, made you decide you wanted to spend the rest of your lives together?"

Shit. That wasn't a question they'd anticipated.

Arkady didn't hesitate, though. "I know it sounds like a cop-out, but—" he looked at Jason "—he's the man I've been dreaming of since I can remember."

He said it with such utter conviction that every reason Jason had not to believe him melted away like ice in the sunshine.

Both Arkady and Christine were looking at Jason now. What had been the question? Oh, yeah, why he wanted to stay with Arkady.

"Because he sees me, 'Flaws and All.'" Next to him Arkady did a double take. "And still thinks I'm worth staying with."

"That was not why I— I never said anything about you having fl—"

"I know." Jason squeezed the hand that was still curled around his. "But I do."

When he turned back to Christine, she was beaming at them and had shoved her keyboard to one side. "To be honest, in light of where you hail from"—she nodded at Arkady—"and of your lightning-quick decision to get married, I had quite the list of questions to ask you two, maybe even separately, but I think we're done here."

Jason blinked. "We are?"

"Is that good or bad?" Arkady asked at the same time.

She leaned back and looked first at Arkady, then at Jason again. "I've been doing this job for thirty years now. I know when I'm being lied to. And if you two aren't head over heels in love with each other, I should probably hand in my resignation right now."

You two? The words echoed in Jason's brain. As in, both of them? Him, yes. He'd seen himself in the pictures, the way he'd been looking at Arkady. He wasn't surprised she'd seen it, too. But Arkady? Arkady was merely a good actor.

Christine got up and came around her desk to shake their hands. "Congratulations on your wedding."

And that was that.

All Jason could do was to follow Arkady to the elevator. He didn't get it. It didn't add up. Arkady hadn't wanted to be kissed that first day. And when he'd decided that sex with Jason was fun, that he, for some weird reason Jason would never understand, actually wanted Jason, he'd made it quite clear that it was just that: sex. No strings attached. Because a deal was a deal.

Jason stepped inside the elevator when the door opened, brain in a chaotic whirl of *buts* and *what-ifs*. When he turned, Arkady grinned at him, one mischievous eyebrow drawn up. He threw a meaningful glance at the camera in the top corner, then crowded Jason against the back wall. "We shouldn't disappoint expectations," he murmured against Jason's lips, whose brain gave up at that point, abandoning him to Arkady's hands and lips, the pressure of that long body, and the bubbles of pleasure fizzing and sparkling through his veins, right down into the smallest of cells.

CHAPTER TWELVE

Arkady nearly floated out of the elevator and onto the street. Part of that was leftover adrenaline from his earlier panic. For a moment there, in the middle, he'd been sure they'd blown their chance. But they'd aced the interview. That was the second part. Well that and the extremely hands-on kiss down three floors that had left both of them breathless. But the biggest part of it was what Christine had seen between them, which neatly fitted the last piece into the puzzle that his talk with Kendra earlier had so very nearly solved. *"He cares too much,"* she'd said. *"About everyone but himself. He thinks he isn't worth caring for."*

And when Arkady had voiced his puzzlement at that, she said, *"C'mon, with everyone walking out on him since the day he was born, then blaming him for his mother's death when he was still a toddler? What conclusions do you think a child can possibly draw from that? How can anything he does ever be good enough to make up for that one terrible sin? Uhm. He's told you about that, right?"*

"Yeah," Arkady had reassured her. And it was true, Jason had, but in typical Jason fashion, of course, where nothing that happened to him was big deal. And Arkady had been too stupid and tangled up in his own insecurities to draw the proper conclusions. But today he had that priceless and elusive commodity: hope.

He signaled his lane change for the exit that would take them down to the ferry dock. The clouds broke, and a wide swathe of sunlight turned the water of the sound a bright silver. It seemed like a sign from the gods that this was an auspicious day to ask important questions.

He glanced at Jason in the passenger seat, who seemed wholly lost in his own thoughts. And that didn't change even when Arkady drove onto the ferry, into their indicated position, and killed the engine.

"Jason?"

"Huh?"

"I need some air. Do you want to come?"

"Yeah, sure." Whether he was absentminded or preoccupied, Arkady couldn't tell.

He led the way up to the observation gallery or whatever they called it, right under the bridge. On a raw day like today it was pretty much deserted. Probably because the wind almost blew them over the railing, but Arkady didn't give a damn. He wanted some privacy.

"Cozy," was all Jason said.

For a while they just stood next to each other, hands on the railing, looking out across the sound.

Then Arkady turned his back on the view. He needed to see Jason's face. "If I get my green card—"

"When."

"What?"

"When you get your green card."

"Okay, fine. When I get my green card—"

"Important distinction."

Arkady briefly closed his eyes and counted to three. "Very important." He paused again to make sure Jason was done interrupting him.

Apparently so, because he was watching a group of seagulls swoop across a spot in the waves.

"When I get my green card, I don't want you to disappear from my life."

Now Jason did look at him, but it was no more than a surprised glance, before he resumed his study of the gulls. "I suppose we can stay friends," he said hesitantly.

"Hell no. You're not paying attention, Yasha. I don't want to be your friend."

Jason's knuckles on the rails turned white. "No, why would you? You'll be glad when you can stop lying to your family. And Vic, and Grigory, and all your friends."

Fuck, this was going all kinds of wrong. "Jason? Shut up. I'm trying to say something. It's important, and I'm fucking it up, and you're not helping."

Jason straightened, almost as if standing to attention, and faced Arkady.

Good. At least he was paying attention now. He was also making Arkady more nervous than he already was.

Right. Here goes nothing. Arkady cleared his throat. "I wasn't lying when I said you're the man I've always dreamed of. I don't want this to be over when I get my green card."

Jason stared at him.

"I don't want to be your friend, Jason. I want to be your husband."

When Jason still didn't answer, Arkady's throat tightened with trepidation. There was a chance that he had it all wrong, of course.

Slowly he went down on one knee, the salt spray that had collected on the deck soaking through his pants. "Jason Cooley, do you want to stay married to me?"

Jason made a choking sound, grabbed Arkady by the jacket, and pulled him to his feet. "May I say something now?"

"I wish you would." Arkady's voice was nearly lost on the wind.

"I have no idea what's going on here, or what just happened, but—" He looked at the water again, as if searching for inspiration, then back at Arkady. "I don't want you to disappear either. But I also don't want you to stay because you think I'll rat you out, or screw you over, or whatever else made you say that just now."

"God give me patience," Arkady whispered under his breath. He took Jason's face between both his hands and leaned in so close that he almost lost focus of Jason's eyes. "Listen, you obstinately self-doubting Thomas: There's only one thing that 'made me say that just now.' You! I want you in my life, because you make me happier than anyone I've ever met. If you're not being too dense for words, that is. You make me feel safe, and stunning, and cherished. You laugh at exactly the right spots. You're sexier than hell, you can drive me out of my mind with one kiss, you have a huge, romantic heart—don't even try to deny it—and I want to show you every day how much of a big deal you are." He ran out of air and gulped in a big lungful. "I love you, Jason Cooley. Don't send me away. Please."

The only thing moving was Jason's Adam's apple as he swallowed. "Are you sure you're talking about me?"

Arkady huffed a laugh. "Yeah, Yasha, I'm talking about you. I'm thinking about you, and I'm dreaming of you. Can I kiss you now?"

Instead of an answer, Jason drew him close and touched his lips to Arkady's, then opened him up for one of those languid, gentle, deep Jason-kisses that curled Arkady's toes and pulled in his ass cheeks.

Jason had to come up for air a few times, but he kept coming back for more, until the announcement over the speakers requested passengers return to their cars.

Arkady was reluctant to let him go; he felt a bit like he'd barely tamed a skittish horse. And he'd completely forgotten that they were, essentially, in public. Kissing. He threw a quick look around, but they were alone.

The wind made their coats crack like whips, and Jason wiped tears off his face. Though whether that was from the wind was anyone's guess.

"Downright punishing, isn't it?" Arkady said.

"Killer. Better head back down."

They returned to their car, and for the next while, Arkady was busy trying not to bump into the car ahead of him as they slowly made their way off the ferry and back to the road.

Once traffic spread out a bit, he said with a sideways glance at Jason, "You okay?"

"Yeah." Jason twirled his index finger against his temple. "Bit busy up here right now." He paused, then tapped his chest with the other hand. "And here too."

"Anything I can do to make it less busy?"

"Not in the car," Jason said dryly.

Arkady laughed. "Now that sounds promising."

They drove in silence until Jason said, "It'll take me a while. You know, to really believe in my gut what you said. I'm trying. Not getting your hopes up is a hard habit to break. Just . . . don't leave, okay? When I— I'm gonna need a little time. I have no idea, though, if it's fair to ask you to stick it out." He leaned his head back and took a deep breath. "Fuck. I'm fucking terrified of screwing this up."

Arkady reached over and put his hand on Jason's thigh without taking his eyes off the road. "Me too. You won't. I won't let you. How about you won't let me either? We'll figure it out. I'm not going anywhere. Not unless you ask me to leave."

Jason shook his head. "Not happening."

"Good. That's good. Man, I'm starving. We should pick up pizza on the way home."

They ate the pizza out of the box at the kitchen table. Arkady was trying his damnedest not to push it, to give Jason the time he needed. Jason made it easy, joking around, keeping the tone light.

Arkady held a slice of pizza out for Jason to bite into.

"Cheesy," Jason said.

"What? Me or the pizza?"

"Both." Jason grinned and took the bite. "You're the cheesiest guy I've ever met," he said thickly.

"Quoth the man who has *Breakfast at Tiffany's* and *Moonstruck* on his shelves."

"Hey, those are not cheesy."

"Romantic?"

Jason scowled at him. "I suppose you wouldn't believe they came with the house?"

"Considering you threw everything else out but the curtains? No."

They grinned at each other. Then Jason said, "So, you and Kendra are ganging up on me."

Arkady froze.

Ripping a piece of crust apart, Jason asked, "You really think coming here would be good for Lily?"

"I think it would be good for both of you," Arkady said carefully. "As for me, I'd absolutely adore having her over." When he didn't receive an answer he said, "Jason?"

"'Jay' is fine. If you still want."

"It is?"

"Mm-hmm. It's what Lily calls me. It's . . . It was too close. I didn't want you that close. It hurt." He was staring at the slowly congealing cheese on the last slice of pizza.

Arkady could practically see the thoughts chasing each other behind his forehead. He swallowed hard and clenched his teeth, so he wouldn't interrupt.

Jason grinned at him. "But you're already doing that Russian thing with my name," he said, twirling his finger at *that Russian thing*. "And you went down on your knees twice." His eyebrows went up in a suggestive arch. "So, I guess we're way past that."

"I guess we are." It was good to be able to breathe again.

"I should probably buy a booster seat."

Arkady's heart sang, and he had a hard time keeping a straight face. "You should."

Jason nodded. "Want a beer?"

And with that, the matter seemed to be closed.

Jason was working two full shifts for the rest of the week and through the weekend to repay swapped shifts, and Arkady spent his mornings lying in wait for the mail truck. Christine might have been on their side, but she could only "recommend." What if someone else disagreed? Arkady had thought he'd had everything to lose before, but the stakes were so much higher now. It terrified him.

When a letter from immigration was finally in the mail, it was only his EAD/AP card. As much as he'd looked forward to being allowed to work, after having already sat the interview, it felt decidedly anticlimactic. And it put him even more on tenterhooks. But at least it gave him something to do. He borrowed Jason's laptop and started scouring job offers and writing applications. He also called Vic to let him know he was legal to work now, and to please let him know about any openings at the college. He still drove to Port Angeles three times a week to tutor Maya, whose English was getting better at a steady rate.

Then Jason had two days off in a row, because his boss had apparently told him he didn't want to see Jason's face anymore until he'd had some R&R.

So they sat over what, for them, was a late breakfast on a Friday morning with the rain sheeting like oil down the window panes.

"What do you wanna do today?" Jason asked with a skeptical glance at the weather.

Arkady, having caught his foot on the floor where the boards were missing one too many times just this morning, took his heart in both hands. "Make no other plans, precious. We're going to Sequim today, to Home Depot."

Jason stilled and cocked his head, listening.

Mug in hand, almost sloshing coffee over the rim, Arkady indicated the hole in the floor. "We'll fix this shit, before anyone breaks their neck."

Jason nodded. "Anything else?" Arkady couldn't tell whether his stillness indicated hope or trepidation.

So he plowed ahead. "We'll do the renos. Make this place ours. Because we live here. Because there's no one here but us who gets a vote as to who belongs here and who doesn't. And you belong here. So, fine, it's not a home yet. But it's about damn time we made it one."

He could almost hear the seconds ticking by until Jason finally set down the mug he'd been holding frozen in midair through Arkady's speech. "I think they're open until nine tonight," he said.

Arkady let out the breath he'd been holding, "You laconic bastard. I'll get you for that."

"Can't wait," Jason countered with a grin.

He didn't fool Arkady, who'd seen the rigidity in his shoulders, the fight going on behind his eyes. But Arkady didn't call him on it. He'd won that fight. That was all that mattered.

They were wandering through the aisles, cart piled high, looking at blinds. They'd both decided the curtains needed to go: Jason, because he wanted to get rid of the last memory of his grandparents, and Arkady, because they were ugly as fuck.

Suddenly a large ad poster for a company that made railings and banisters stopped Arkady dead in his tracks. It had a picture of a stairwell with a long wooden slide running alongside the stairs between two floors. "Oh my God. Jason. We need something like that. For Lily. C'mon, man. She'll love it. Hell, I wish my own ass was narrow enough to go down on that. It's glorious."

"I have some glorious suggestions about what you or your ass can go down on, but it doesn't involve slides."

Arkady did an involuntary roundhouse check, before looking back at Jason. "Jesus, God, be a little careful." He was only half-serious, though. His heart was already beating faster at Jason's *glorious suggestions*.

"Don't worry. No one's listening." Jason seemed to consider the poster. "It has potential," he conceded. "But if we want to do something for Lily, setting up a room for her should have priority, don't you think?"

"Yes," Arkady breathed, heart in his throat. That sounded like Jason wanted to make his daughter's visits a regular thing.

Jason nodded. "Definitely worth keeping in mind though. The slide."

They brought their haul home with a stop for beer on the way, and threw themselves into their home improvement project with a minimum of coordination needed. Jason started on the floor, and Arkady on the lighting over the breakfast bar, for once in his life happy to be an electrician. They worked in companionable silence until the streetlights came on. Then Arkady straightened and stretched a kink out of his back. "I'm hungry. What do you say I go get us some dinner?"

Jason took a screw out from between his teeth. "Good plan. I'm about ready to eat anything that isn't moving."

Arkady went to get them both burgers and fries and picked the mail up off the floor on the way back in.

One of the letters was from USCIS. Warm paper bag in one hand, mail stack in the other, he tried to run his thumb over it to feel for a card. Nothing. They were kicking him out. His fairy tale was over. Cold and hot at the same time, he didn't even bother to remove his jacket, just dumped everything he held on the kitchen table and cut the envelope open with the carving knife.

Jason stood slowly and laboriously up from the floor, watching his every move. "What?"

Arkady unfolded the letter and read the first three lines twice before he finally trusted his voice enough to read them out loud: "'Welcome to the United States of America.'" He could hear the disbelief in his own voice as he continued. "'This is to notify you that your application for permanent residence has been approved. It is with great pleasure that we welcome you to permanent resident status in the United States.'" Excitement started to bubble through his veins. "Something, 'important number', something . . . Here: 'We will soon mail you a new Permanent Resident Card. You should receive it within the next three weeks.'"

He finished the rest of the letter in silence, about the status being conditional for two years, which they'd known, and to apply for removal of the conditional status before the two years were up. Then he dropped the letter on the table and threw himself at Jason, wrapping his arms around Jason's neck. "'Approved'!" he yelled. "'With great pleasure.'"

He started dancing around the room, because he couldn't contain his joy while standing still. All the while Jason was watching him with the strangest expression on his face, half smile, half tortured tension.

"Approved," Arkady said again. "We should stage some kind of celebration. Thanksgiving, maybe? Seems appropriate." He got carried away with his own plans. "Do you think Kendra will let Lily stay with us for Thanksgiving? Or is it a big family thing, like Christmas? Oh, that reminds me, what are we going to do for Christmas?"

He ran out of steam when Jason didn't say anything, but when he turned, a tentative smile was slowly spreading across Jason's face. "You're really staying, then?"

Arkady stopped short, then crossed the room in three long strides, and took Jason's face between his hands. "Of course, I'm staying, Yasha. I told you. Family. One day you're just going to have to believe it."

"Yes. I will. I do." The smile was happier now, but still a tad uncertain.

"I've thought of an excellent way to claim this house, by the way," Arkady said with a salacious wink to lighten the mood. "You're going to fuck me in every single room. I was originally thinking, when we're done renovating. But we can start right now. I don't mind a little dust."

Jason took a deep breath, then let it out slowly. "You are so on."

"Don't move. I'll get the goods." Arkady raced upstairs for condoms and lube. When he came back, Jason was indeed standing in the same spot.

"We both took a medical, do we need condoms?" he asked.

Arkady inhaled sharply. "I don't."

"Me neither."

The condom package went sailing onto the table, and Arkady wiggled the lube bottle. "This, though."

"Oh yeah, tons of it," Jason agreed. "Because I think it's my turn."

The room instantly turned several degrees warmer. "Are you saying what I think you're saying?"

Jason grinned. "I'm saying you have way too much fun getting fucked for me not to at least try it."

Arkady's throat was very dry, suddenly. "Oh, you got it, *solnishko*," he whispered. "Now kiss me. Breathing is overrated."

Jason pulled him close with one finger by the waistband of his jeans. Which did funny things to Arkady's toes. Then Jason did kiss him, which did funny things to the rest of his body, especially his brain. He had no idea how long they stood like that, but by the time they came up for air, he was on fire and ripping the clothes off his body.

Jason did the same, then pulled Arkady close again, pressing their bodies together skin to skin. He didn't seem to have a single thought for the fact that part of his skin was black gel liner.

Arkady counted that as a win, then he stopped thinking, because Jason bent him over backward and sucked on his nipple, then licked a line down to his navel.

For a second, Arkady felt himself falling backward, but then his ass touched the armchair. He arched his back over it laying himself open to Jason's hands and tongue and lips. But he let out a surprised shout when those lips closed around his dick and Jason started sucking him in. *Jesus, God*, he was going to lose it.

He tried to protest, but no sound came out; tried to grab Jason's head, but bent over backward as he was, couldn't reach him, and his abs had inexplicably turned to jelly. Jason was a natural, and the fucker had a rough tongue that did— *Sweet Jesus!* Yes, exactly that.

He started floating, and did his best not to, because if Jason wanted to get fucked, he needed to hold it together, but then that thought, too, was gone. Wave after wave of pleasure washed through him, carrying him further and further along, until their energy crested and collapsed, leaving him panting and limp, and vaguely aware of Jason's arms pulling him up and around and cradling him in his lap.

"Sorry," he murmured. "I lost it. You have one talented mouth."

"Talking of which, as distracting as you are, that mouth needs to eat."

Arkady huffed a laugh, but dragged himself upright. "So mercenary."

They sat across from each other at the table, buck naked, Jason as tense as Arkady felt pliant. He'd forgotten how hungry he was until he took the first bite, then he was ravenous. He polished off his burger in a few large bites, and practically poured the fries from their container straight into his mouth. Sated in every way, he licked his lips, then got up and prowled around the table until he stood behind Jason. He dug all ten fingers into Jason's shoulder muscles and got a tight groan in return. "Come on, big guy. Let me see how decorative *you* are bent over that chairback."

Jason promptly stood up and went to lean against the chair.

"Oh, no," Arkady said. "The other way around. I want your ass in the air."

Jason drew a shuddering breath, then turned and let his upper body fall forward into the seat.

If Arkady had worried that, having just come, he'd be out of the game for a while, he needn't have. Just the sight of Jason's ass and those powerful thighs was enough to get him interested again.

He gave Jason a pile of pillows to lean on so he wouldn't pass out head-down in the middle of the action. "Legs as wide as you can," he commanded, and Jason complied, his heavy balls giving Arkady all kinds of ideas. He filed those away for later and poured a generous amount of lube into his hand. He cupped Jason's balls, then moved his hand upward, spreading lube all along Jason's ass crack. A tremor ran through Jason's thigh muscles, and, damn, that was hot too.

Arkady poured more lube, lined his dick up in Jason's crack, and rocked gently up and down across the hole, getting himself hard again.

Jason had both hands curled around the armrests and was breathing audibly.

With a step back, Arkady spread Jason's ass cheeks, then bent over and blew across the little star-shaped pucker, watched Jason's glutes clench and relax.

He spread lube over his fingers and ran his index finger across the place. Same result. He pressed down on the tight muscle and started massaging it with his thumb.

With a loud groan, Jason relaxed, and Arkady got his index finger in. More lube, and slicking the finger in and out had Jason tighten his hold on the armrests, fingertips denting the soft material.

Arkady pushed his finger in all the way and crooked it slightly, pressing down. Jason twitched as if electrified. Jackpot.

"Oh God, sweet Lord," Jason breathed when Arkady started finger-fucking him with well-controlled pressure. He listened to Jason's breathing getting ragged, then pulled his finger out and lubed himself up, pouring more lube on Jason's ass for good measure. First time and all that.

He jacked himself a few times, groaning with anticipation and the slick friction of his own hand, and then with the pressure of Jason's ass against his glans. Slowly, ever so slowly, he inched past the first barrier, and with a little gentle rocking, past the second. Then, knowing exactly where the sweet spot was, he kept his strokes shallow, making sure to hit it with every forward motion. Happy that he'd come earlier and had all the time in the world now, he set a steady, deliberate rhythm, watching the sweat run along Jason's spine and into his hair, watching his knuckles turn white on the armrests.

At some point Jason began to curse, a constant, inventive stream of expletives that furthered Arkady's knowledge of the English language to no small extent.

Then Jason started begging, and that finally kicked Arkady off his plateau. He watched Jason fall completely and utterly apart under him. It was the most erotic thing in the universe, and it pushed him inexorably farther toward his own edge. He sped up and thrust deeper until his body was slapping Jason's ass with every move.

When his balls tightened, he curled his fingers around Jason's dick and started jacking him, concentrating on Jason, delaying his own orgasm by a few heartbeats, until Jason's staccato breathing told him he was close. Then he allowed himself the staggeringly sweet release.

Jason was only a few seconds behind. His whole body jackknifed into the chairback, then slowly relaxed in a long shudder, interrupted by a number of smaller tremors.

Arkady massaged the long muscles in Jason's back, then helped him stand up. It was a good thing, though, that they merely had to twist and take a half step to collapse on the couch.

Occasionally another small spasm still ran through Jason's body, before his breathing slowed to normal and he wrapped one arm around Arkady's middle and rested his head on Arkady's chest. A low chuckle rumbled through his body. "That chair'll never be the same again."

Arkady grinned under the arm he'd thrown across his eyes. "I hear jizz is good for leather."

They both started laughing, though neither had much breath for it. Then they simply lay there for a while, not talking, just listening to each other's heart beat.

"The answer is yes," Jason said suddenly into the darkness. "I do want to stay married to you."

Arkady's smile nearly split his face, and his free hand caressed the side of Jason's face, his jaw, his neck, until he felt himself drifting off to sleep.

He was almost gone when he heard Jason's sleep-heavy voice mumble, "Thanksgiving, huh?"

CHAPTER THIRTEEN

They were going to pick up the turkey on their way back from the airport. Jason threw a glance at his watch. If Arkady's parents ever made it through customs, and they all ever got out of here, that was.

Arkady had opted for a precooked turkey from the get-go—the man knew his limits. But Jason, seduced by the idea that maybe he could have that elusive experience, a traditional Thanksgiving dinner, had actually started to google turkey recipes. It hadn't taken him long, however, to realize that the arcane instructions—what the hell was *brining* or *basting*—were best left to acolytes. Arkady was right; for the uninitiated, it was a recipe for only one thing: a disaster.

He checked his watch again. *Breathe, Cooley.* They had ample time. Nothing to be nervous about. Except meeting Arkady's parents, of course. Jason tried to tell himself that, having nothing to offer meant he could just lean back and relax. Impressing parents was impossible at the best of times. He was here to make this an amazing visit for Arkady, because Arkady was looking forward to their visit. That was all that mattered. And, man, was he ever.

Arkady'd been fidgety all week and had buried himself in work, prepping like a demon for his new job at the Russian Community College. He was prowling in front of the gate like a tiger now, ready to pounce. As Jason watched him, his body suddenly straightened and his arms shot up in a wide wave, which was answered by a tall, lanky man and a tiny woman coming through the door: Nikolai and Alina, Arkady's parents.

Arkady somehow managed to wrap himself around both of them at the same time, and was enveloped in answering hugs that dissolved into kisses, shoulder slaps, and reassuring touches on arms and chests and faces, luggage forgotten at their feet.

Jason couldn't remember if he'd ever tried to hug his parents, but probably not. The concept was too alien. He hung back, wanting to give the three of them as much privacy as possible before the inevitable round of awkward introductions, but Arkady was already waving him over with that slight dip of the head that said, *Come on, what are you waiting for?*

As it turned out, there were no introductions, or none that Jason caught, anyway. There was only the same consummate hug for Jason that Arkady had received earlier. It didn't feel as awkward as Jason had expected, but it threw him off-kilter, regardless. Or maybe *because*—it was too unexpected.

Nikolai held him by the shoulders for a moment and beamed at him, his eyes a little paler than Arkady's, but equally frank. He said something in Russian to Arkady, then, with a slap on the shoulder and a laugh, let Jason go.

"He says, he knows American men don't kiss to say hello, and that he hopes he's greeted you properly," Arkady translated with a wink.

Jason gave a thumbs-up all around, then snatched up the two big suitcases, leaving them to deal with the smaller items. Since he didn't understand anything, it was easy to ignore what sounded like polite protest behind him as he headed out.

Having stashed everything and everyone in the car, he drove, so Arkady would be free to chat and point out landmarks and contort backward in his seat almost constantly.

Occasionally Jason's eyes met Nikolai's in the rearview mirror, and he knew himself watched and silently evaluated.

Precooked turkey loaded in the back, they made their way to Natalya and Anna's place, whose guestroom would be the parental quarters during their stay. They'd all agreed on a quiet evening in, to give everybody a chance to catch up, or indulge their jet lag. Though, as Anna whispered to Jason, when he and Arkady finally said their goodbyes after midnight, "Man, it's hard to keep up with Russians partying."

Lily, Kendra, and Dan came to town the next day, and Lily immediately dragged her parents upstairs to show them *her* room. Arkady and Jason had put the finishing touches just a week ago, and though Lily hadn't seen it completely finished in person, they'd kept her involved with pictures and chats, so she could choose colors and themes she liked. She'd considered it her room since they'd first started, and couldn't wait to sleep in it. Arkady had told Jason in no uncertain terms that the slide was next and that they'd have to finish it in time to be her Christmas present.

Arkady's parents, Anna, and Natalya arrived about an hour later, and the silent and staid house of Jason's childhood disappeared forever, conquered by laughter and voices; food was being piled onto the table and breakfast counter, beer cooled and wine opened, and Lily slid the banister blank until she was called to dinner.

Jason didn't even try to follow the Russian part of the conversation, though he nodded and smiled when he caught Yelena's name, and guessed that Arkady was telling his parents about Jason's new line of work. Yelena had recommended him to friends and business partners; she'd also taken Jason aside and told him bluntly that he needed to hire a guy she knew to design him a website, and that he'd better triple his price if he wanted to be taken seriously. He'd done both and was now slowly pulling in business; enough that he'd cut down his work at the studio to one shift. All because Arkady had known what he was good at better than he had himself. He met Arkady's gaze across the table and quickly concentrated on the sweet potatoes Kendra had brought to the feast, to get past the sudden tightness in his throat. Seriously, while gratitude was what Thanksgiving was all about, there was no reason to get all mushy over it.

Nikolai said something that made Arkady roll his eyes and Natalya burst out laughing. "Papa likes you," Arkady growled. "He says previous experience with my choices made him set his expectations low, but that due to some miracle, I seem to actually have found a good man, and that I'm to stick with you." His eyes were full of light, giving the lie to his injured tone.

Jason barely managed to swallow the needy, *Yes, please*, that was on the tip of his tongue. "He only thinks that because he doesn't understand a word I'm saying," he quipped instead.

"Well, I understand you just fine," Natalya cut in, "and I agree with him—it's a freaking miracle." Arkady mimed flinging mashed potatoes at her from his spoon, and Lily giggled.

Jason ducked low over the table, made sure everyone had what they wanted, and tried to keep the bowls and glasses full, and Arkady happy. That last part was easy. Arkady was juggling several conversations in two languages while teaching Lily the Russian words for the foods on her plate; a blind man would have been able to see that he was in heaven. Jason found it hard to tear his gaze away from him long enough to get more beer from the kitchen.

He grabbed the cold ones and straightened up to find Nikolai standing next to the fridge, handing him reloads. They silently exchanged bottles, and when Jason had closed the door, Nikolai pointed at Arkady, then at Jason and back at Arkady. "Good," he said, raising his bottle in a toast. Jason hurried to open one for himself and raised it in answer, then hid his blush behind a deep gulp. Nikolai snickered and returned to the table. Jason stared after him for a heartbeat, then followed him, bemused. What the fuck had just happened?

As per Lily's decree, they played Jenga after dinner, until her eyes started drooping and Arkady dragged her upstairs and put her to bed. Natalya broke out a bottle of vodka, which some of them ended up drinking from coffee mugs because there weren't enough glasses.

When Arkady came back, he caught Jason around the middle, kissed him, and flashed him a big contented smile. "See? I'm still here. You're stuck with me now." A thousand thank-yous and I-love-yous danced in his eyes, making Jason feel warm and amazing and powerful.

As weird as their thrown-together, sharing-a-child-with-his-ex-and-her-husband family was, it seemed to be what Arkady had been looking for and what he needed. And Jason was the bridge that connected them. He was good for someone after all.

He belonged here. With Arkady.

"I know." He tapped his chest. "You're stuck right here."

Dear Reader,

Thank you for reading G.B. Gordon's *Operation Green Card*!

We know your time is precious and you have many, many entertainment options, so it means a lot that you've chosen to spend your time reading. We really hope you enjoyed it.

We'd be honored if you'd consider posting a review—good or bad—on sites like **Amazon, Barnes & Noble, Kobo, Goodreads, Twitter, Facebook, Tumblr,** and your blog or website. We'd also be honored if you told your friends and family about this book. Word of mouth is a book's lifeblood!

For more information on upcoming releases, author interviews, blog tours, contests, giveaways, and more, please sign up for our weekly, spam-free newsletter and visit us around the web:

Newsletter: tinyurl.com/RiptideSignup
Twitter: twitter.com/RiptideBooks
Facebook: facebook.com/RiptidePublishing
Goodreads: tinyurl.com/RiptideOnGoodreads
Tumblr: riptidepublishing.tumblr.com

Thank you so much for Reading the Rainbow!

RiptidePublishing.com

ACKNOWLEDGMENTS

I owe a debt of gratitude to everyone who shared their experiences about getting a green card through marriage, and the fears and hopes the process entailed, especially for a same-sex partnership.

Many thanks as always to Margaret, my indomitable checker of everything plot and word related, and to Y, for time and space and love.

Santuario
The Other Side of Winter
When to Hold Them (A *Bluewater Bay* Story)
Bluewater Blues (A *Bluewater Bay* Story)

ABOUT THE AUTHOR

G.B. Gordon worked as a packer, landscaper, waiter, and coach before going back to school to major in linguistics and, at thirty-five, switch to less backbreaking monetary pursuits like translating, editing, and writing.

Having lived in various parts of the world, Gordon is now happily ensconced in suburban Ontario with the best of all husbands.

Website and blog: gordon.kontext.ca
Twitter: twitter.com/gb_gordon
Goodreads: goodreads.com/gbgordon
Facebook: facebook.com/gb.gordon.5
Instagram: instagram.com/g.b.gordon

Enjoy more stories like
Operation Green Card
at RiptidePublishing.com!

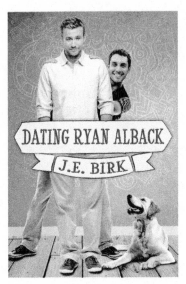

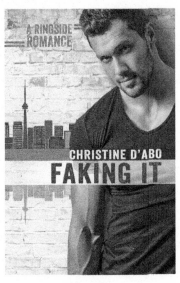

Dating Ryan Alback
ISBN: 978-1-62649-537-1

Faking It
ISBN: 978-1-62649-553-1

Earn Bonus Bucks!

Earn 1 Bonus Buck for each dollar you spend. Find out how at
RiptidePublishing.com/news/bonus-bucks.

Win Free Ebooks for a Year!

Pre-order coming soon titles directly through our site and you'll
receive one entry into a drawing for a chance to win free books for
a year! Get the details at RiptidePublishing.com/contests.

2

CPSIA information can be obtained
at www.ICGtesting.com
Printed in the USA
LVOW03s1752060218
565498LV00003B/545/P